THE STRONG ROOM

A Golden Age Mystery

R.A.J. Walling

Spitfire Publishers

Copyright © 2023 Spitfire Publishers LTD

First published in 1927 by Jarrolds, London. This edition published by Spitfire Publishers LTD in 2023.

*To
FVW*

CONTENTS

Title Page
Copyright
Dedication
About 'The Strong Room'   1
Part 1 Mr Colebroke Disappears   5
Part 2 Mr Grainger Makes a Discovery   55
Part 3 Adventures of Mr Pinson   93
Part 4 A Reconstruction   157
R.A.J. Walling Crime Fiction Bibliography   190

ABOUT 'THE STRONG ROOM'

Noel Pinson, barrister and sometime amateur sleuth, savoured his carefully made cup of tea in his digs near the Temple, London's legal district. Waiting for him in the morning's post was an important envelope. The letter inside outlined the curious disappearance of English country solicitor, Westmore Colebroke. Colebroke had vanished three-months ago, the morning after he had arranged with his financier a large withdrawal of funds.

Aided by retired detective superintendent Joe Grainger, Pinson works to solve this puzzling case traveling from London to Devon, Paris and Morlaix in Brittany. Has Westmore Colebroke met with a violent end? Was it a coincidence that both his office clerk, Toms, and chauffeur, Julep left his employ just before the hapless lawyer disappeared? And why didn't Colebroke fit the mould of a staid provincial solicitor?

About the Author

R.A.J. Walling was an English crime novelist and West Country newspaper editor. Robert Alfred John Walling was born in Exeter in 1869, and between 1927 and 1949 he wrote twenty-eight detective novels. He was especially popular in the US, the prestigious New York publishing house, William Morrow & Co, publishing most of his books. Wallings's novels were also translated into French and Italian by leading European publishers. He is best known for his serial character, Philip Tolefree, a private investigator masquerading as an insurance agent, who starred in twenty-two books. His other serial characters, Noel Pinson, an English barrister and amateur sleuth and retired detective superintendent Joe Grainger featured in Walling's first published detective novel, *The Strong Room* (Jarrolds, London 1927). Pinson and Grainger had previously teamed-up in several serial-only detective stories written by Walling, *The Fatal Glove* and *The Fourth Man*. Walling died in 1949 at his home in Plymouth, South Devon, aged 80.

Praise for the R.A.J. Walling

The Strong Room
'Unusual and rather horrifying' *The Times*
'An original and uncommonly well-written detective story' *Bookman*

The Dinner Party at Bardolph's: A Detective Story
'An unusually well told murder mystery' *New York Times*
'Solution – complete surprise' *Sunday Chronicle*

Murder at the Keyhole
'Exceptionally well told and skilfully constructed... satisfying and interesting to the last word' *New York Sun*
'Has far more movement and bustle than most tales of this kind' *J.B. Priestley*

The Man with the Squeaky Voice
'Ingeniously contrived... make room on your shelf' *New York Times*

The Fatal Five Minutes
'A thoroughly satisfying detective story' *Times Literary Supplement*

Behind the Yellow Blind
'R.A.J. Walling's best stroke is keeping his "master-mind" so cleverly concealed' *Evening Standard*

Follow the Blue Car
'A mystery story of first-rate quality' *New York Times*
'Keeps the reader thrilled and bewildered almost to the last page' *The Spectator*

The Tolliver Case
'One of the best "puzzlers" that Mr Walling has written' *The Scotsman*
'A delightful story' *New York Times*

The Five Suspects
'Told with all the narrative skill for which R.A.J. Walling is famous' *New York Times*

The Corpse in the Crimson Slippers
'A master in the creation of an atmosphere of expectancy that it is difficult to put this book down' *Times Literary Supplement*
'A book for those who like difficult and intricate puzzles' *New York Times*

The Mystery of Mr Mock
'An entertaining and very competent piece of work… Walling's clues are puzzling yet credible' *The Times*
'The best book Walling has given us' *The Observer*

Bury Him Deeper
'One of the best of the many good stories that R.A.J. Walling has written' *New York Times*

Dust in the Vault
'Probably the most puzzling case that Philip Tolefree has ever undertaken' *New York Times*

They Liked Entwhistle
'Well written, skilfully plotted… rattling good tale' *Chicago Tribune*
'A necessity for all discerning fans' *New York Herald Tribune*

Why Did Trethewy Die?

'By far the best of the Tolefree stories and not far from the most baffling and most logically constructed mystery of the current year' *New York Times*

By Hook or by Crook
'Has the authentic Walling touch. And that means that you will not want to miss it' *New York Times*

Castle-Dinas
'A beautiful structure of mystery and bafflement' *New York Times*
'A Godsend for top-drawer mystery fans' *New York Herald Tribune*

The Doodled Asterisk
'Tolefree–a skilled bloodhound… the detective work is up to the Tolefree standard' *New York Times*

A Corpse Without a Clue
'One of the most puzzling crimes with which Mr Tolefree has dealt' *New York Times*

PART 1 MR COLEBROKE DISAPPEARS

I

Mr Noel Pinson awoke on a June morning with a sense of immense well-being.

In the course of a satisfactory night's sleep he had enjoyed a highly satisfactory dream, in which the Lord Chancellor had caused the letters "KC" to be added to his name, and, with the rapidity only observed in dreamland, he had just been appointed Lord Chief Justice after serving about five minutes in the office of Attorney General.

Yawning and rubbing his eyes beatifically, he became conscious that it was Irene who had put an end to his meteoric judicial career by letting up the spring blind with a rush. He saw the tail of her skirt whisk out at the door.

She had placed his tea and his letters on his bedside table.

He was not Lord Chief Justice Pinson; he was not even the Rt. Hon. Sir Noel Pinson, KC, HM Attorney-General, nor even Noel Pinson, KC, hoping to get a Recordership in a year or two. He was Noel Pinson, *tout court*, a junior counsel of great merit and some popularity but limited connections.

Still, it was a June morning. The sun shone into his little bedroom in the cramped little flat in the Adelphi, where he lived because it was so near The Temple and saved travelling expenses. He had slept well. His tea was ready. Life was tolerable.

He made his first cup with care. It was an old habit of his bachelordom to begin the day with a carefully made cup of tea. He sipped and savoured it in a mood of lazy enjoyment, and prepared its successor before he took up the letters.

A bill. A handsome offer from a capitalist to lend him any sum he fancied up to ten thousand pounds, without vexatious inquiries about his capacity for paying it back. He put them aside with some other missives in halfpenny envelopes.

An offer of a brief in a county court case. A cheque from a firm of solicitors. Good.

And, last, a thick-feeling envelope in an unfamiliar handwriting, postmarked "Longbridge."

Pinson found himself saying, "Longbridge! Where the deuce is Longbridge?" as he slit the envelope with the handle of his teaspoon. He unfolded a letter of four sheets of thick paper and turned it over to look at the signature.

"Ah, good old Elburton!" he said. "Of course—Longbridge, I remember."

At the reading of the first sheet Pinson sat up straight in bed. At the second the legs of his striped pyjamas were over the side. At the third he was standing barefooted on the carpet. When he came to the signature, "Yours sincerely, Francis Elburton," he had his feet in slippers and was hitching down a dressing-gown from a peg.

Mrs Pinson's door was on the other side of the flat. Two steps and he was knocking on it.

"Good morning. Lady Pinson," he said as he entered. "I hope your ladyship has slept well. And how is the Honourable Dora Pinson this fine morning?" he added, going to the cot where a young person of three had been recumbent, but was now upstanding, holding out her arms and ingeminating "Dada!" He took her.

"What is the new game, Noel?" his wife asked. "You seem in high spirits."

"I am. I have had a perfect night. Before the inevitable and heavy-footed Irene woke me up I was already trying on the full-bottomed wig of the Lord Chief Justice. Irene is fatal to other delicate things besides your china. But I have a sense of adventure upon me, Mrs Pinson. I am convinced that things are going to happen."

"Seeing as how, I suppose, you have received a letter with news. A good brief?"

"No such luck. But it may be more interesting than most briefs. If you can remember how we both felt—let's see, was it four years ago? When we were in that Fallofield affair with the joyous Joe Grainger—you may guess how my perverted mind is working now. You know, I missed my vocation when I went in for the law. I ought to have been at Scotland Yard. The very scent of a mystery excites my nostrils to quivering. Read that!"

He sat by his wife's bedside while she read the four paged letter.

"Read it out," said Pinson, "so that the Honourable Dora may share our excitement. I like to hear things read: they sound different. You hear shades which your eyes miss."

"My dear Pinson," she began to read.

"Yes, yes; but always begin at the beginning of every document. I haven't got the atmosphere if you don't show me where it was written. I want to see the man writing it."

"Oh, very well . . .

"57, High Street, Longbridge,
"June 4.
"MY DEAR PINSON,
"I don't make any apology for writing to you though we have had no communication for a long time. You remember that when we met at your Club three years ago I told you I had taken over the management of a quiet country branch of the Bank. I think I may have mentioned that it was here at Longbridge.

"Anyhow, here I am, and have been, in a rather nice old bankhouse with a good garden, ever since my wife died. My daughter keeps house for me, and we are naturally not inconsiderable personages in this sleepy little town.

"I am greatly afraid that its somnolence is going to be broken unpleasantly very soon, and that is why I write to you. I recall the part you played with Grainger in bringing to light the facts of the Fallofield affair, and I want your help in this.

"One of our greatest friends in Longbridge was Westmore Colebroke, the solicitor. You may never have heard of him, though he had a rather high reputation in the West. An admirable fellow—to all my knowledge, as straight as a die—and a really interesting man.

"Well, Colebroke has disappeared. Without rhyme or reason, between night and morning, he is gone—vanished as utterly as if he had never existed. The circumstances are peculiar. It is not, or does not appear to be, a police matter—at any rate at present. But I cannot rest for my fears and suspicions. Three months have passed already. I have waited in the hope of some natural explanation of the strange facts. I can wait no longer without setting on foot more expert inquiry than I am capable of. I do not want to create a public sensation and attract a horde of newspaper men. Will you come down and help me?

"I won't say anything now about fee or reward: I know your temper. But for heaven's sake put off every other obligation and tell me I may expect you here at once.

"I hope you will be my guest. You will find the place quaint and pleasant.

"Yours sincerely,
FRANCIS ELBURTON."

"Dora," said Mrs Pinson, "your Dada is going to desert us. He thinks he is called Vidocq or Sherlock Holmes or Crutchett, or something, and he's going away to do detective stunts for a nasty old man down in the country called Elburton."

Miss Pinson, playing with the cord of Mr Pinson's dressing-gown, looked wise but said nothing.

"It sounds interesting," said Mrs Pinson. "Who is Elburton?"

"An old sobersides who was in his last term at St John's when

I first went up. I forget how we knew each other. He married very young and instead of embarking on an adventurous and ambitious career leading to Capel Street or Wormwood Scrubbs, the budding financier settled down to penal servitude as a bank officer. I believe his gaolers think very well of him, but when his wife died he insisted on going away in the country to pine for her. Strange, nice chap."

Mrs Pinson's eyes went soft for a moment.

"And the lawyer—Colebroke?"

"Just heard his name: that's all," said Pinson.

"You'll go, of course?"

"With the assent of the future Lady Pinson and the Honourable Dora—but you'll not withhold it. Think of the advantage of having two strings to your beau! If the Lord Chancellor should unaccountably fail to do his obvious duty by me and leave me to pursue the stony road of the all-but-briefless barrister, what a priceless thing to be able to step in and take charge of the CID when they have their next internal row. And now, Honourable Dora, go to your mother. It's me for the bathroom."

II

"It's the strangest thing I ever encountered, even ever heard of."

The prematurely grey-haired man of forty-three who sat opposite Pinson at the dining-table pushed across the port and taking a pipe from his pocket slowly filled it.

Pinson nodded, took a cigarette from the box and lit it. From the drawing-room came the sound of a piano.

"Very strange, I admit," said Pinson, "but I think it has been worrying you, Elburton. Unduly, I mean. Shall we go and have some music with Miss Maud now and take the story tomorrow?"

"Why, no!" the grey-haired man replied. "I must get it off my chest, Pinson. It's only the keeping it in that worries me. That's the reason why I sent for you. It won't take long to tell. Maud shall play to you afterwards."

Pinson rose from the table and with a "May I?" stretched his legs in a long chair. "Fire away then, Elburton."

He sent his cigarette rings floating to the ceiling.

"Westmore Colebroke was, as I told you, my closest friend in Longbridge. He——"

"By the way, Elburton," Pinson interrupted. "How many people know that anything is wrong?"

"None—but me. At least, I think none but me. That is part of my trouble, Pinson. It's my secret, which I acquired in the way of friendship and business. I cannot tell whether I have done right or wrong to keep it."

"Speaking from a long acquaintance with the law-courts, my dear Elburton, I should say that it's always right to say nothing. But that is a generalisation. Go on."

"Colebroke was my friend. When I came here, Pinson, I was heartbroken. I asked the Bank to give me a quiet place. I wanted to brood. I brought my girl to this old house with the idea that she might make some respectable acquaintance and that I might be free to nurse my sorrow. I was morbid. No doubt about it. One of my greatest debts to Colebroke was that he stirred me out of my morose way of life. Woke me up. Gave me interests. Colebroke was an able man—quite a good lawyer, I believe. He was in demand all over a large district. Had a big practice. But he was a lot more than that—a bit of a scholar, for instance. We talked books and movements. Often got up enthusiasms, just as we did in the old days up at Cambridge. He had his education on the Continent. He cultivated the humanities. Fond of music too. He loved to come and hear Maud play. . ."

"Bachelor?" asked Pinson.

"Yes, and every day of thirty."

"Ah! . . . Well?"

"We found our tastes assorting then. And we became close friends. There were never any secrets in my life—till now. He knew everything there was to know about me. All his financial interests passed through my hands: I thought I knew all there was to know about him. You can find out other characteristics as you go along, Pinson; but have you got his figure in your mind by now?"

"An exterior figure—yes. There he is, on the mantelpiece."

"Ah—I forgot," said Elburton. "Yes, that's a photograph—the last one of him."

"He looks more than thirty," Pinson observed.

"It's the beard. He picked up the fashion of beard-wearing in his student days in Paris and he never shaved. He had many little foreign ways: they were part of his charm perhaps. He would break out into little snatches of student songs. If Maud got hold of the air of some chansonette he was delighted."

"I see," said Pinson. "Now can we come to the crisis?"

"Yes—about three months ago. No, not quite. It was on the 18th March. Colebroke came to me in the morning and said he had need of a large sum of money . . ."

"Now," said Pinson, "nous y sommes! Be careful now, my dear Elburton, will you? Consider yourself in court. Recall exactly what was said and give me the conversation in the first person."

"Very well; I'll try. Colebroke came to me in the morning—at eleven o'clock, and said, 'How much is there in my current account, Elburton? I want a rather large sum, and I want it in notes.' I had his passbook made up. He'd made some big lodgements lately, and we had discussed the question of investments but decided nothing. The balance turned out just to top three thousand pounds. Colebroke said, 'I thought it would be about that. Can you give me the lot in notes?' I could not. I said, 'I can send into Westport for the cash, Colebroke, and get it through by this afternoon. It's rather a big lot for us here.' I thought it strange that he should want so much money in such a form, and I suppose I showed my surprise, for he said, 'Thanks, Elburton. Will you do that? It's for a very special reason.' He gave me a draft, and I promised to let him have the money before three o'clock. He called at the bank and took it away with him."

"What were the notes?" asked Pinson.

"Thirty hundred-pound notes and a small balance in lesser ones. Before he left, Colebroke asked if I was disengaged that evening and whether Maud would be home. If so, he would like to come in for some music. I said I should be delighted. He came after dinner, about half-past eight. Maud played for him. He smoked his pipe, seemed in good spirits, sang a little, begged for chansons, was very grateful to Maud for a jolly evening, had a drink, shook hands with us both, went home about eleven—and I have never seen him since, nor has anybody else."

"Wait a minute, Elburton," said Pinson. "I want to rub all that in."

He sat contemplating the ceiling for a few moments, puffing his cigarette.

"Extravagant man, this Colebroke?" he asked.

"Not a bit. A wealthy man. Lived very simply. Invested much money. Had a large income from investments and made a big thing of his profession."

"Where did he live?"

"In another such house as this—not far down the street. His office on the ground floor, facing the street. His rooms above. Behind, a large garden very like mine."

"Keep a big establishment?"

"No. A housekeeper. One maid. He had a chauffeur-gardener sort of man, who left his service about that time and was thought to have sailed for Canada. Colebroke was looking about for somebody to take his place, but he had not found his man."

"What about his relations or connections?" Pinson asked.

"That's the strangest thing of all," Elburton answered. "So far as I can discover, Colebroke had not a single known relation in the world. His father, whose practice he inherited, was an old man, a widower soon after Colebroke was born—his only son. The father was an only son also. So it comes about, Pinson, that there is nobody to inquire into the disappearance of Colebroke except myself, and up to the present I am the only man who knows that he has disappeared."

Pinson raised his eyebrows.

"Then, my dear Elburton, you have evidently been lying overtime for the past two or three months, eh?"

Elburton rose and paced the room.

"Yes," he said, "it is on my conscience."

"The first person who came to you next morning, of course, was Colebroke's housekeeper, knowing that he had been with you overnight."

"Yes, and if she had not been a particularly stupid old woman I should not be in my present awkward position. She did not understand my first reply—that I didn't know anything about Mr Colebroke's whereabouts. Then I remembered the withdrawal of the money from the bank, and jumped to the conclusion that his disappearance must have something to do with his 'very special reason.' And in a fit of recklessness—to dodge the servant's questions—I said he had doubtless been called away suddenly to London. She understood me to have stated this as a positive fact, and told everybody so. I left it at that. And out of it all my trouble has grown."

"But I say, you know, Elburton!—although that may have been good enough for a stupid housekeeper, it wouldn't satisfy his office staff."

"It all fitted in diabolically. Colebroke was a terrific worker himself, and he kept only one clerk, a man named Toms. That clerk left him the week before. He had told me his successor was coming from London immediately."

"No inquiries from the successor?" Pinson asked.

"Not a word: I haven't seen a shadow of him."

"And you have naturally had to tell the same lie to tradesmen, and clients, and every sort of inquirer?"

"To a few would-be clients. But here is the mystery, Pinson. Before he vanished, Colebroke had cleared up every bit of business he had in hand, to the last shred. He had no client outstanding whose affairs were not in final and perfect order. He had some time before disposed of every scrap of estate business that might have hung on after his departure. He had paid every tradesman to the last penny. His servants always had a month's wages in hand. So that until now my unintentional lie has had a perfectly good currency. I have even paid another month's wages to the servants—professedly on the instructions of Colebroke. And everybody now is under the impression that I am in communication with him."

Pinson pressed the end of a cigarette into the ash-tray.

"You must have been precious fond of this man, Elburton."

"I liked him, Pinson."

"If you did not more than like him, my dear fellow, you are the most fearful ass in Christendom."

"Why?"

"Not for a man that one merely likes does he deliberately put his neck in a noose. Think what would happen if it should be found that Colebroke had met with foul play. Where would you be, with these pretences and evasions and this assumption that you were in touch with him?"

III

Elburton ceased pacing. He pulled up in front of Pinson's chair.

"My dear Pinson, I have thought! Since the idea occurred to me that Colebroke may have met with a violent death, I have thought of nothing else. That's why I wrote to you. That's why you're here. I'm in a devil of a mess, and I don't know how to get out of it. For the last week life has been almost intolerable. Maud had begun to notice my state. I could not endure to have her worried about me or about anything else. Pinson! she's all I have. You must help me for her sake."

"Steady, Elburton," said Pinson. "Sit down and take it quietly. No emotion. No sentiment. Just cold thought. Let's think it out."

The host got back his self-command with an effort and seated himself again on the opposite side of the table.

"Thanks, Pinson," said he. "I could kick myself, but the fact is that ever since the idea of Colebroke's possible death occurred to me I have been in a fever. I have been quite incapable of cool thinking."

"Quite so. I understand. But now you've got to get your temperature down and reason this out. There's plenty of time.

If no discovery has been made in three months, it's not likely that one will be made now unless we make it ourselves. Nobody suspects. The comfortable theory is accepted that Colebroke was called to London and has since been summoned abroad. Let that do—for the public. But we, Elburton, have got to get to work on all possibilities. Is the man alive? And if so, where is he? Is he dead? And if so, where is the corpse?"

Pinson eyed his companion steadily. Elburton winced and shuddered.

"I hate to think of Colebroke in that way," he said, with a glance at the door.

Pinson's glance followed, and came back to Elburton's face. He was silent for a few moments. Then,

"Reach me a cigarette, Elburton. Thanks. Now—are you perfectly candid with me? Have you told me everything bearing on the disappearance? Or are you hiding something?"

"I think not. May I ask why you ask?"

"Certainly. You hate to think of Colebroke in connection with certain possibilities, and as you tell me so your thoughts fly to the drawing-room and your eyes follow them . . ."

Elburton flushed and bit his lip.

"You don't think me indelicate?" Pinson asked. "If so, I drop the question."

"No, no!" cried his friend. "I have appealed for your help, and of course you must know everything. But in any inquiry you make, for God's sake, Pinson, spare the feelings of my girl."

"Ah," said Pinson. "Stop a moment. Stop more than a moment. Think hard, Elburton, and when I ask you the inevitable question tell me the absolute truth. There must be no reservations between us. If there are, then I have never heard of the existence of Mr Westmore Colebroke and I go back to London by the first train tomorrow."

Elburton sat resting his head in both hands. Pinson silently smoked. The sound of the piano came faintly through the walls. At last Elburton looked up and said,

"Ask me the question, Pinson, whatever it is."

"The inevitable question is this: if I begin this inquiry, am I to go on with it whatever I find?"

The banker looked staunchly in Pinson's eyes, drew his shoulders tight and clenched his hands.

"Yes," he said, "whatever you find."

"Then we'll go and join Miss Maud in the drawing-room. We've left her alone an unconscionable time."

Pinson rose. Elburton stood between him and the door.

"A minute, Pinson," said he. "You'll do nothing if you can help it to destroy the happiness of that girl?"

"Nothing whatever, willingly. But I should certainly be in a better position to avoid a false step if I knew what is in your mind about her, Elburton. Tosh! Of course I know. But why don't you say yourself?"

"What do you suspect then?"

"My dear fellow, it's no case of suspicion. The thing is as plain as a plate. You know that Miss Maud was in love with Colebroke. You were hoping that your daughter and your friend would have made a match of it. You hoped it right up to the time of his disappearance. What you do not know is whether Miss Maud has information which you do not possess. You are afraid to ask her. Am I right?"

Elburton drew back while Pinson was speaking and sank into a chair.

"Yes," he said. "You are right. Almost as if you had been inside my head. Am I so blind? Is it all so plain to an outsider as that?"

"Quite," said Pinson. "It's written all over the place in letters two feet long. But cheer up, Elburton. Why take so comparatively small a thing so seriously? Nobody is going to accuse Miss Maud of having spirited Colebroke away! Why can't you ask her what she knows—if she knows anything?"

Elburton did not answer immediately.

"Very well, my dear fellow," said Pinson. "Don't worry about it. I know why. There are some things in a girl's life which her father cannot approach, and an unhappy love-story is one of them . . ."

"Unhappy!" cried Elburton.

"Yes—unhappy. How can it be otherwise when it ends like this? Colebroke could never have returned her love, and she could never have told it."

"Oh, but Pinson! You are utterly wrong! I don't think anything had ever been said. Maud is very young. There was plenty of time. But I know certainly that Colebroke was passionately in love with her—passionately. And she—I think she greatly admired him, perhaps loved him. Their tastes were so well assorted, though their ages were not. You are wrong: there was no unhappiness in the story."

"Anyhow," said Pinson, with a smile, "I have got it out of you. My dear Elburton, you would make a perfect victim of the smart cross-examiner if ever you got into the witness-box. It was a little unfair of me, perhaps. But also perhaps it was the least brutal way. I understand your father-feeling. I have a daughter too—though, thank heaven! as yet too young to raise any such problem in my breast. I am forgiven? Good! Now I assume, under all the circumstances, that you have carefully avoided giving Miss Maud any inkling of your doubts and suspicions?"

"Yes," said Elburton, "she is under the same impression as everybody else—that Colebroke is away on business and that I am in communication with him."

"Of course," said Pinson. "Now shall we join Miss Maud?"

The piano-playing had stopped. When they reached the drawing-room a tall slim girl stood with her back to them looking through the long window over the rambling garden that stretched away from the house in a maze of little lawns and beds and paths to a forest of fruit-trees. She turned to greet them with a momentary smile in her brown eyes. A lithe figure, a broad brow, a thoughtful air, a dark complexion smooth with youth. Pinson amused her with some badinage about the difficulty he had experienced in dragging her father away from the wine, and his own breathless anxiety to join her for the tantalising music he had heard in the distance. While he rallied them both, Pinson observed the girl with curiosity. Here, he reflected, was possibly the heart of the mystery of Colebroke's disappearance.

A quiet girl of strong feeling, he thought. A girl who, if her affection were engaged, would hold securely. A little old for her age—she was not more than twenty—but that was probably due to her lonely life with her father and the early responsibilities of housekeeping. A girl who, if she found a congenial soul, would go out steadily to meet it. He wished he knew more of Colebroke: the photograph of the bearded man who might have been any student of the Sorbonne did not tell him much, except that the type was not characteristically English. It was the artistic type. Maud Elburton had none of the stigmata of that type, except the broad brow which revealed her musical feeling. Music had probably brought them into touch.

"We've been talking business a long, dry time," said Pinson. "Now won't you play or sing us something?"

Almost reluctantly she went to the piano. Pinson followed her across the room and turned over a pile of music on a stool.

"Ah," he said, "here's an old friend I'm rather surprised to meet!" And he began to hum,

"Autour du chat noir
A Montmartre le soir.

But, my dear Miss Elburton, how on earth..."

The girl laughed.

"Not very edifying, I suppose, but our friend Mr Colebroke is fond of the tune and he brought it over for me to play."

"Colebroke?" said Pinson, with an air of puzzledom. "Ah yes, Elburton—that's the solicitor friend you mentioned to me. Exotic taste for a country lawyer, eh? But then you never know what we lawyers are up to, do you, Miss Elburton? We're a sad lot. I should like to meet Mr Colebroke some time."

"He's away now," said the girl, turning to the piano and fingering the notes. "I'm sure he would be glad to know any friend of Dad's."

IV

Mr Pinson woke, stretching himself after a night of profound slumber. He missed Irene with his tea, but was soon down in the old garden breathing the air of another perfect June morning.

He blew a kiss vaguely to the eastward in the direction where he assumed Mrs and Miss Pinson to be sleeping. For it was early. Mr Pinson appeared to be the only person waking in Elburton's house.

The strains of a song were echoing in his ears:

"Autour du chat noir
A Montmartre le soir."

When had he heard that rather ribald ditty before? It was being howled by a crowd of young men in an obscure little café in one of the narrow streets that surround the Marché St Honoré. Quite appropriate to that scene and to those singers, keeping time by hitting the heels of their glasses upon the table tops. But he had never come across anything more incongruous than that song in the repertoire of a particularly charming English girl in the sedate drawing-room of a bank manager in an English provincial town.

She was a charming girl, this Maud of his friend Elburton's. Ingenuous, intelligent, fresh and merry.

Yes, merry. That was one of the things that puzzled Pinson. She was, according to her father, in love with this strange being Colebroke. Yet the circumstances of his sudden disappearance had not affected her gaiety. Was she in his secret—if he had a secret? Or did she merely place a blind trust in her father's tacit assurances that he knew Colebroke's whereabouts and was acting for him?

Her father was an ass! That's what he was—a dear old priceless ass who, in a mixed and woolly emotion of friendship for this solicitor chap and consideration for his girl and hatred of fuss, had got himself into a particularly nasty mess. And everybody else. A nasty, tangled mess.

Mr Pinson did not quite see how he was to start extricating

Elburton from the mess. He found a seat under a west wall, sat down to bask in the sun, and did some thinking.

About Elburton first. It was the very devil for Elburton, this business. His folly in keeping up the pretence of his knowledge of Colebroke's movements hampered the inquirer enormously. In fact there could be no open inquiry without betraying Elburton, and even a whisper in public would blast him. Who would trust a bank manager caught lying under such circumstances? That was a snag—an ugly snag.

About this Colebroke. Pinson was not a very staid and conventional person himself. But an English provincial solicitor. Come now!—he should be a man who shaved clean, had a certain conservatism of outlook, a certain formality of manner, and an absolute rigidity of conduct. He might be allowed a little sardonic sense of humour. But he must be set square on his feet, which should be encased in solid boots, and he should avoid Bohemian tendencies as the plague. If there were any highly-coloured episodes in his extreme youth he should bury them at the bottom of a respectable-looking deed-box which was never on any account opened. He should . . . inspire confidence. Yes! that was the exact phrase: he should inspire confidence.

Now how could a person of the quality of this Colebroke inspire confidence? He wore a beard—at his age! He looked (in his photograph) like a vivacious and handsome student of the Sorbonne instead of looking (as a provincial solicitor should) like a grown-up English schoolboy of Methodist parents. What did a solicitor want with beards and big neckties and Bohemian songs? If he had even been near the Chat Noir or any other such pleasaunce he ought to conceal the disreputable fact from everybody else, and forget it himself if he could.

And yet—Pinson thought—there was something rather attractive about the fellow, if one could divorce him from his job and forget that he advocated or solicited or conveyanced or attorneyed.

He was a bright spirit, this Colebroke; he had charmed Elburton and infatuated the girl. What was the secret that had moved him to this disappearance?

"This, my dear Pinson," he apostrophised himself as he lit a cigarette to aid reflection, "is a problem which you will never solve by discursive speculations on the character of a man you never saw. You will have to reduce it to its simplest elements and then proceed objectively."

Pinson got up and addressed the bench on which he had been sitting.

"Very well," said he. "I agree. Let us have the elements."

In the simplest form they were contained in two questions:

Is Westmore Colebroke dead?

Is he alive?

If he were dead, Pinson reflected, then the problem was that of a mere crime, and it could be solved by the ordinary means of investigation—if the folly of that dear old ass Elburton had not made investigation so hard.

But why should he be dead? There was no corpse, and no trace of a crime, no suggestion of a motive.

Let us suppose he was alive. Why should he disappear? There might be a thousand reasons. Never mind them. How did he disappear?

Pinson took a turn up and down the path, returned, and shook an admonitory finger at the bench.

"Pinson, my dear fellow, you are going too fast. The first question is. Has he disappeared? No, there is even a prior question to that: Can he disappear? Is it possible for a man—even the most solitary—to wipe out all traces of himself and vanish from the knowledge of his fellow men beyond discovery? You do not think it is, Pinson. You are perfectly certain that, however clever he may be, the man is bound to leave some clue by which with patience and skill he may be traced. Therefore, Pinson, if Mr Westmore Colebroke is still alive in the world, it is up to you to find him."

He resumed his promenade. The facts Elburton had put before him convinced him that Colebroke had some urgent reason for getting out of Longbridge and leaving behind him not a scrap of information which would indicate his whereabouts. More than that: he had taken care to rouse no suspicion of an intention to depart, and had acted precisely in his own routine way up to the last moment.

But he had been aware for some little time that he might have to go, and had made the most careful preparations to avoid an immediate inquiry into his absence. For—

He had got rid of his chauffeur-gardener, and while affecting to engage another had clearly taken no steps to that end.

He had so adjusted his professional engagements that no client would be seeking him immediately after he had gone.

His clerk had left him a week before, and he had engaged no other.

He had completed or transferred all outstanding business and paid all debts.

Therefore, when Mr Westmore Colebroke said goodbye to the Elburtons that night, he knew that he had at least a week or two's start of any enquiry that might be set on foot. It was a very deliberate disappearance with intent to leave no trace and to make the task of discovering him as difficult as possible.

"But, my dear sir," said Pinson, pulling up before the bench again, "there is one most important element in the problem that you have overlooked up to now. Colebroke, as a solicitor, frequently had engagements in London which took him away for a few days at a time. All solicitors have. Would it not have been much simpler and much less surprising for him to announce to the Elburtons and tell his housekeeper that he had an appointment in town, depart for London in the usual way, and vanish from there? My dear Pinson, where are your wits? That's the first corner you must get round."

It took Pinson several turns up and down the path to work out the point. Colebroke had certainly made elaborate preparations during two weeks—perhaps more. He must therefore have known that he might go away suddenly. But when? Did he know when? Or did he even know for certain that he would go? That could not be determined. But on the actual day of his disappearance he suddenly knew. He came to Elburton for a large sum of money. He wanted it at once, and in notes. But a man might suddenly want money in that form for several reasons. There was blackmail, for example...

Even so, it would still have been an easier and a simpler and more probable course for him to have told the Elburtons and his housekeeper that he was going away to London. Why not? Why, even at the last, even at the Elburtons' door, did he not say that?

Pinson stopped at the bench.

"Can't you see?" he said to himself. "It's as plain as Irene! Even when Colebroke said goodbye to the Elburtons and walked down the street he was not quite certain that he would have to go. My dear Pinson, you may depend upon it that the critical moment which determined the whole thing occurred between the time when Colebroke left this house and the next morning. You have to discover what happened in those few hours. When you do that you will discover Colebroke."

At the end of this soliloquy Mr Pinson bethought him of breakfast and returned to the house.

V

"Had Colebroke any close friends besides yourself, Elburton?"

They were talking in the bank manager's private office after breakfast.

"I don't think he was intimate with anybody. Of course, he knew everybody and everybody knew him. As he was a bachelor he did very little entertaining, and though he went to many people's houses he was really only on family terms, so to speak, with us."

"That's as to Longbridge," said Pinson. "But how about the big town?"

"Oh well, of course," Elburton replied, "he was a great deal in Westport. His practice in the courts was mainly there, and he was a member of the Westport Club. But I don't think he was particularly warm with anybody there. I never heard him speak of any such friendship. In fact, I believe his principal chum in the place was a little fellow named Lebaudy, who keeps a fruit store on the Eastern Quay and does a big trade with early potatoes and strawberries from France in the summer and onions in the winter. Quite a character. How Colebroke picked him up I don't know. But he was very fond of talking French with anybody who would, and especially French slang. Lebaudy has a wonderful vocabulary of it."

Pinson's eyes narrowed as he looked away from Elburton through the window, which gave a view down the garden. Miss Elburton was walking there, employing a pair of scissors among the roses. A time began to run again in Pinson's ears. He got up suddenly.

"Well, I mustn't keep you about in business hours, Elburton. I'm off on the prowl. Don't take any notice of my movements. If I'm not back to lunch or dinner, never mind. I don't know where I may prowl. And of course you won't let on to anybody that I have any interest in Colebroke? I'm just a guest of yours. I may pretend to other people that I am his long-lost cousin or I may affect not to know of his existence. It all depends. Au revoir."

He went out humming,

"Autour du chat noir
A Montmartre le soir."

and wandered down the quiet High Street of Longbridge. It was a wide, pleasant street, lined with old houses, mostly Georgian; it had grown in the eighteenth century and suddenly stopped growing in the nineteenth; but some of the buildings were older, with thick cob walls, and here and there a roof of thatch survived.

The inn was The George. It stood back with a cobbled courtyard before it, and a pole on which hung a portrait of King George the Third almost obliterated by the sun and the rain. Just beyond the inn was a large building, rather neglected, in grey limestone, under which the pavement passed beneath arches. In the arcade a doorway was plastered with official notices about swine fever and other dismal scourges, market bye-laws and warnings to all and sundry against committing nuisances. It was a moribund market hall.

Pinson stood for a moment in the shade of the arches and looked out into the sunlit street. Exactly opposite was a house almost a replica of Elburton's. The lower windows were obscured by wire blinds, and on a brass plate at the side of the door appeared the legend:

COLEBROKE & COLEBROKE
SOLICITORS
COMMISSIONERS FOR OATHS

Pinson took a good look at the house. Like Elburton's, it had a good room on the first floor, running the length of the building, with three generous windows. Venetian-blinds were closed inside them. Above were bedrooms, and in the roof three dormer windows of attics.

Pinson went across the street and pulled a bell. It jangled at the back, some long distance away. He heard footsteps on stone passages. The door was opened by a neat maid.

"Is Mr Colebroke at home?" Pinson asked.

"No, sir. He is out of town."

Pinson put on his most winning smile—the one that could always charm Irene to unheard-of exertions in the way of tea-making.

"How unfortunate!" he said. "I had very urgent business with him. Do you know when he will be back?"

"No, sir. Perhaps you would like to speak to Mrs Paddon."

"Mrs Paddon?" Mr Pinson queried, his eyebrows going up.

"The housekeeper, sir."

"But what about his managing clerk?"

"Oh, Mr Toms, sir, he left a long time ago, and now there's nobody. But you had better see Mrs Paddon. Please to step inside."

Mr Pinson stepped inside and at the girl's suggestion took a seat in the lobby of the clerk's office while she went to fetch the housekeeper. But as soon as she had gone he left the seat and made a rapid tour of the offices. They were barren. Old auction bills on the walls, an almanac or two. In the clerk's den a tall desk with a rail above it, account books, a few tin deed boxes, a few volumes of the Law Reports.

Mr Pinson lifted the cover of the tall desk and looked at its miscellaneous contents—blotting paper, note-heads, tape and sealing-wax. He picked up a small notebook, ruffled the pages, and glanced at figures on one or two. As he heard footsteps on the flags of the passage, Mr Pinson dropped the cover of the desk and absent-mindedly put the little notebook in his pocket.

When Mrs Paddon appeared with a curtsey Mr Pinson was sitting where the girl had left him, playing tunes with his fingers on the handle of his stick.

"Ah, Mrs Paddon—good morning," he said, bringing the smile into action again. She was a buxom woman of forty-five, very prosperous-looking.

"Good morning, sir."

"My name is Pinson, Mrs Paddon." He ingratiated it as if she had a right to know all about him. "I am a barrister. I had some little business with Mr Colebroke and I am disappointed to learn that he is out of town. The girl could not tell me when he would be back. She suggested that I should see you."

Mrs Paddon moved a pace or two before she replied.

"I'm sorry, sir, I can't tell you. Mr Colebroke has been away for some time and is detained on important affairs. It is uncertain when he will return."

"Dear, dear. That is a great pity. Let me see, when do the judges go the Western Circuit? Is it next week? But perhaps I oughtn't to bother a lady with these details." Pinson's smile was at its zenith.

"Oh, not at all, sir. I'm accustomed to it. Yes, I believe the assizes begin at Winchester next week, and the judges will be at Exeter the week after. But I did not hear Mr Colebroke say that he had any cases this circuit."

"No, no. It wasn't a question of a case, Mrs Paddon. You know we barristers aren't allowed to—but there, I needn't trouble you further, if Mr Colebroke is not likely to be back. But—how long has he been away? Do you know his London address? I might have seen him there if I had only known it."

"No, sir, I have no address. But you might get information from Mr Elburton at the Bank, sir."

"Mr Elburton! You astonish me, Mrs Paddon. Why, I needn't have bothered you at all if I had only known. How vexatious! I am staying with my friend Mr Elburton. So I will take myself off. Curious that I should not have mentioned it to him. What lovely old houses these are," he added, casting an admiring glance at the antique auction bills "So roomy."

The housekeeper bridled with pleasure. "Yes, sir, they don't build such houses nowaday."

"Wonderful! Wonderful!" said Pinson. "I do admire a good building. With all this space you must have some fine rooms above."

"Yes, indeed, sir. Two beautiful rooms on the first floor. If you are interested—perhaps you'd like to have a look at them?"

"Oh, but it's a shame to give you so much trouble!" Pinson smiled furiously.

"Not a bit of trouble, sir. Come this way."

Mrs Paddon threw open a wide door at the head of the staircase. The dining-room. A little awkward to have a dining-room so far from the kitchen, but Mr Colebroke had put in a lift to save their legs. The room overlooked the garden at the back. It was a sitting-room as well, she explained. There could be no drawing-room on account of the space wanted for offices. That was why Mr Colebroke's piano was in this room. Mr Colebroke was very musical.

Pinson adequately admired the apartment.

Mrs Paddon produced a bunch of keys from under her apron, and unlocked a door on the opposite side of the landing.

"This is Mr Colebroke's office."

Pinson heaved the breath of a man who had breasted the tape

at the end of a race.

The long room with the three windows looking out over the street to the market-hall. It was pervaded by a greenish light on account of the venetian-blinds. Mrs Paddon raised two of them, but had some difficulty with the middle one. Pinson came to her aid. The cord had broken, and one of the slats was fractured. She had not noticed that. The blinds had been kept drawn because of the power of the summer sun.

Never mind, said Pinson. There was light enough.

"A fine room—oh, quite good."

He repeated his praises in a variety of forms as he paced it from end to end. The inner wall was quite covered with bookshelves, only broken by the doorway. At one end a deep fireplace. At the other the oak panelling which filled the spaces between the windows was repeated on a larger scale, and in the centre was a portrait of an elderly man with grave, strong face. Pinson stood looking at this picture, then turned to Mrs Paddon with a lift of the eyebrows.

"Mr Colebroke's father, sir," she said. "A very fine gentleman. I came into his service as a tweeny maid just after he was married. A very fine gentleman."

"Ah," said Mr Pinson, "so in a sense you are a family retainer, Mrs Paddon. He looks rather—what shall I say?—rather sad."

"Yes, sir. He never got over the death of his wife. He had only one joy in life, and that was his son, Mr Westmore. He called him back from Paris when Mrs Colebroke died, and they two were like brothers, sir. And I will say that two nicer gentlemen never lived."

Pinson turned from the picture and eyed the housekeeper closely.

"Is Mr Colebroke like his father?" he asked.

"No, sir. Not a particle of resemblance. He is the living image of his mother. She was a French lady—and, though French, a perfect lady, if I may say so."

Pinson paced the room from end to end once more. Then he thanked Mrs Paddon for her courtesy, hoped to see her again when Mr Colebroke returned, and took his leave.

He crossed the street to the arcade of the market hall for another look at the exterior of Colebroke & Colebroke's, solicitors, etc., and then strolled to the hotel.

VI

That afternoon a car engaged at the hotel called at the bank-house for Mr Pinson. He left while Elburton and his daughter were taking their coffee after lunch.

"Well, Maud," her father asked her, "what do you think of my friend Pinson?"

The girl clasped her hands in front of her—a little trick of hers while pondering—and paused a second or two before answering.

"I think," she said, "he's rather nice. Yes—very nice. And amusing. But——"

"Yes?" Elburton asked as she lingered. "Let's have the feminine reservation."

"But I think he is inquisitive. No—that's not the word. I can't think of the right one. Observant, perhaps. Yet more than that. Very clever, I should say. Is he a successful barrister?"

"So so, I expect," said Elburton. "The profession is overcrowded, you know. But Pinson will do with half a chance. What made you think him inquisitive? Did he cross-examine you?"

"No. He has hardly asked me a question; but he seems to have his ears pricked up all the time. He looks exactly like a man with an urgent mission. Is he down for anything special, Dad?"

"Eh?" Elburton started. "No—nothing special. He was very glad to come down for a rest and to renew old memories with me. I met him at his Club two or three years ago, and recently something reminded me of him and I wrote to him. That's how it came about."

Elburton stumbled hesitatingly through this account, and closed his eyes a moment to pray that it sounded more convincing to Maud than it did to him.

She seemed to notice nothing faulty in it.

"I'm very glad you had the idea. Do you know, since he came you've been ever so much brighter? You seemed worried the last few weeks, as though you had something on your mind. I expect it was my dull company."

Elburton turned away to find his pipe on the mantelpiece.

"My dear Maud," said he, "that's a strange fancy, old girl. You know I want no company—but you'll make me sentimental. There's nothing for me to worry about, except to give you a good time. Now—do you know? I thought you had been feeling a bit 'fed-up'—as you say—these last few weeks."

"So you got Mr Pinson down to 'unfeed' me! Thoughtful old Dad!"

"Oh," said Elburton, "you mustn't count too much on Pinson. He's an erratic sort of person, and will be on view or not, just as the fancy takes him."

"Never mind. I don't want any society but yours, and I'm not fed up, and you're not to worry about me, and I'm quite all right. So be off to your stuffy old office, and I'm going for a walk."

Elburton watched her dance away and stood looking for a minute or two at the doorway through which she had passed. He drew his hand across his eyes. "That girl! If she only knew!"

Mr Pinson was very busy making an undying friend of the driver of the car that took him to Westport—the Ford which was the only hiring car Longbridge boasted. Mr Pinson always proceeded on the assumption that anybody might be useful to him at any moment—especially a good driver. Also, he had a strong liking for his fellow men. Therefore he exerted himself, his smile, his facetious tongue, his ingratiating manner, to bind that jarvey to him with links of steel. Incidentally, also, to extract from him any scraps of information that might possibly be serviceable.

It was easy to make insulting reflections on the character and performances of Tin Lizzies in general, but to except from the general denunciation of the genus this particular specimen, which seemed to be wonderfully good, probably because she was so skilfully handled.

Cobbledick didn't know about that. (Pinson had soon discovered that his friend the driver was called Cobbledick.) But Mr Pinson manifestly rose several points in his estimation through this piece of discrimination.

Mr Pinson supposed that there wasn't much motoring in Longbridge. It didn't look like a place where many cars were kept.

Cobbledick confirmed that observation. Of the five cars which resided in Longbridge he knew the ownership, the pedigree, the quality and the age of every one. He recounted them. There was his own. There was the grocer's and the doctor's and old Mrs Pethybridge's, the widow who lived down by the bridge, an ancient limousine which her gardener ill-treated, and there was Mr Colebroke's two-seater, and that was all. And the only one of them that was any good was Mr Colebroke's two-seater. As for that, Cobbledick would say that it had been well looked after, though it was by a dirty dog if ever he should say so. How a gentleman like Mr Colebroke could have put up with such a dirty dog so long he, Cobbledick, could not imagine, and it was a good riddance to Longbridge when the dirty dog took his scowling face and his bitter tongue away to annoy the inhabitants of Canada.

At the end of this speech Cobbledick paused to take breath.

"Phew!" said Mr Pinson. "I should rather guess you aren't very fond of Mr Colman's chauffeur, Cobbledick."

"No, I ain't, and that's flat," said Cobbledick. "It's Mr Colebroke, sir, not Colman."

"Oh, well—Colebroke. Is he a local tradesman?"

Cobbledick turned a glance of pained surprise on Mr Pinson and jerked open the throttle a fraction.

"No, sir. Young Lawyer Colebroke—as fine a gentleman as ever was. I did think of applying for the job, but he wanted a man who could do a bit of gardening as well, and I ain't no gardener, worse luck. But if he do go on trying to drive that bus himself he'll come to grief. I never seen such drivin'!"

Pinson smiled encouragement to the critic.

"Mr Colebroke, sir—he do seem to think a car's like a donkey: the more you beat him the better he goes. There won't be no car left if he goes on drivin'. But there, he's away and the bus is having a good long rest."

Mr Pinson proceeded to encourage the garrulity of his companion.

"Don't you think it curious, Cobbledick," said he—as who should consult a philosopher—"that a man who treats his engine well should fail to treat his fellow men well? This chauffeur of Mr Colman's now—I beg pardon: did you say it was Colson?—no, Colebroke: this chauffeur of Mr Colebroke's, now. He must have been a bad hat to make you hate him; yet he was a fine driver, you say?"

"Curious? Yes, in a way. Tell you what, sir—I hated that man Julep like poison: he were a poisonous creature that I wouldn't trust with a worn-out oilcan. Yet he had a regular love of his engine—a born engineer. I believe he and Mr Colebroke had a 'ell of a row (beggin' your pardon, sir) before they parted, and Mr Colebroke, he told him off that powerful you would think he'd have slinked away and never showed his nose again. Yet he couldn't keep away from that there engine. I seen him loafin' about the garridge a day or two after he was supposed to be gone to Canada. He reg'lar loved that car. He treated it better'n if 'twas a human bein'. An' yet the man had no feelings—a dirty swine who couldn't treat a dog kind-like. I 'ate a man who carries an ammonia squirt to fire off at dogs. You're right, sir; 'tis curious."

Mr Pinson, during this speech, seemed to be startled by several objects that they passed on the road. He jumped and fidgeted. At its close Mr Pinson's eyes were full of inquiry. But he confined himself to one remark.

"I shouldn't think your Mr Colefield would like to have a discharged chauffeur about the garage, Cobbledick."

"Oh, as to that, sir, you may be sure Mr Colebroke didn't know nothing about it. And, as a matter of fact, since Mr Colebroke's been away I haven't seen nothing of Julep. That's three months agone or more, and I suppose he's out in Canada by this time. Here we are, sir. Where would you want to be going—what part of Westport?"

"You shall drop me at the Royal Hotel, Cobbledick, garage the car, go and get some tea when you like it, and be ready for me at six o'clock. How about it?"

"That'll be quite all right, sir."

It was half-past two. Mr Pinson entered the hotel and went to a telephone box. He selected a number from the book and got through to it.

"That Mr Grainger's?" he asked. "Oh, Mrs Grainger. Mr Grainger at home? Yes, I'll hold the line. . . . That you, Grainger? I'm Pinson. Very kind of you. I'm glad to hear your voice too. Eh? Oh, just a holiday. I'd like to shake hands. Think Mrs Grainger would give me a cup of tea if I looked round? I thought she would. . . . Very well, then; I'll be there at five o'clock. By the way, Grainger, nobody else in Westport knows I'm here on holiday. You understand? Righto! Cheerio!"

Mr Pinson then went to the smoke-room and ordered a drink. He told the waiter that he did not mind in the least having a soft drink, as no hard drinking could be done after two-thirty. But he would like a little writing-paper, and if there were no other candidates for soft drinks in the smoke-room for half an hour so much the better.

Mr Pinson sat at a copper-topped table with a pad of notepaper and a pen in his hands. He used one side of a sheet only and made the following entries:

Colebroke . . . Lebaudy . . . Toms . . . Julep.
Lebaudy . . . Chat noir.
Toms . . . where?
Julep . . . Liverpool.

On the other side of the half sheet, Mr Pinson drew a rough plan of two rectangles of unequal size. One he marked "9 paces"; the other "12 paces."

Next he rang for the waiter and asked him to bring a local time-table. In this he inspected the list of trains from Westport to London. He took another half sheet and made some further entries:

Westport 12.15 midnight; Paddington 7 a.m.
Transatlantique: Westport 12 to 4 a.m.; Le Havre 5 to 9 a.m.
Westport Shipping Co.: Westport 2 a.m.; St Brieux 4 p.m.

He added this document to the other, finished his drink, and stalked up and down the room in thought.

VII

At four o'clock Mr Pinson boarded a tramcar outside the Royal Hotel, and at a quarter past he was strolling along the Eastern Quays, watching the business of unloading small coal steamers and taking general cargo out of coasting packets.

He liked the pleasant bustle, the plash of water against the walls, the acrid smell of sun-heated water, the puffing of donkey engines and the rattle of chains.

He liked the babel of voices—broad West-country words, the clipped Doric of Scottish gangers, the pungent eloquence of the gods of justice at the weighing machines.

But above all he seemed to like the sharp clatter of sabots across the granite setts and the railway lines, where men in blue blouses and elaborately patched trousers plugged to and fro between a little steamer and a grey limestone warehouse, carrying bags of potatoes into store. Along the front of the warehouse was painted the legend:

CIE. ANGLO-FRANÇAISE DE LEGUMES ET FRUITS
JEAN-MARIE LEBAUDY
SUCCURSALE À SAINT BRIEUX.

Mr Pinson lingered here for several minutes, observing the operations and glancing at the warehouse entrance, where a florid gentleman of ample proportions with a fine jet-black beard burst occasionally into explosions of vituperation, of which the wearers of the blue blouses took not the slightest notice.

One of them pulled up near Mr Pinson to wipe the sweat off his forehead. Mr Pinson said to him, "Salut! Fait chaud."

"Bougrement chaud," said the blue blouse.

"Oh, oh!" said Mr Pinson, laughing and clapping his hands to his ears.

"Pardon," said the blue blouse.

"N'importe," said Mr Pinson. "Est-ce qu'on y trouve le patron?"

"C'est bien lui," said the blue blouse, pointing to the florid gentleman with the black beard.

Whereupon Mr Pinson walked up to the warehouse and raised his hat to the black beard.

"Pardon, monsieur," said he. "Have I the pleasure of addressing Mr Lebaudy?"

The black beard in turn raised his hat with a ceremonial sweep and replied,

"The pleasure is all mine, sir."

Whether Mr Lebaudy thought Mr Pinson the possible purchaser of a large consignment of potatoes could not be determined from his manner. If he did, Mr Pinson immediately undeceived him.

"My name is Pinson, Mr Lebaudy," said he. "I have the advantage of you, for of course you have never heard of me, while I am charged with a message to you from Paris."

"Ah, là, là, là! From Paris? How interesting," said Mr Lebaudy. "Will you come inside, Mr Peenson?"

He led the way into an office glassed off from the store, kicked a bundle of newspapers off a wooden chair, upon which he invited Pinson to sit, and perched himself on a high stool.

"From Paris? Voilà! And who is it that is so good as to remember me in Paris?"

"That is the strange thing, Mr Lebaudy. I can't remember his name—for the life of me I can't recall it."

"Vottapitty!" exclaimed Mr Lebaudy, or so it sounded to Mr

Pinson. "Quel dommage, done!"

"Ah, yes! But you will enable me to remember it when I tell you," said Pinson. "You know the Marché St Honoré?"

"If I know the Marché St Honoré!" cried Mr Lebaudy. "As you English say, I should smile, what!"

"Well, off the Marché St Honoré, there is a little street goes away to the left towards the Avenue de l'Opéra, I think."

"Tiens!" said Mr Lebaudy. "I should smile, what! There are a dozen streets."

"Ah yes!" said Pinson. "But this one has three cafés in it."

"They all have three cafés," said Mr Lebaudy, "if not six!"

"Really? Well, I can't remember the street or which café it was; but I was there with some friends who introduced me to the patron, and in the course of conversation I happened to mention Westport. 'Oh, Westport,' says the patron, 'do you know Westport?' 'If I know Westport!' says I. 'An old friend of mine is at Westport,' says he; 'do you know him—Monsieur Lebaudy?' 'No,' says I, 'I have not that pleasure.' 'Ah,' says he, 'when you are in Westport again, ask for Monsieur Jean-Marie Lebaudy and give him my warmest salutations.' 'I will,' says I. But, monsieur, can you believe it? I left without ever knowing the name of the café, and I have forgotten the name of your friend."

Mr Lebaudy pulled his beard reflectively.

"Who would it be that should send me greetings?" he ruminated. "I know so many. There is Jacques Dupuy at the Coq d'Or, and old Père Buisson in the Rue St Hyacinthe—but he's been cleared out to make room for an hôtel, and Jules Armand at the Samaritain—but oh, it is despairing. I cannot tell."

"Perhaps I can help you a little," said Mr Pinson. "It was a place where they talked a good deal about an Englishman who lived in Paris up to seven years ago—I've forgotten his name. He was a regular customer, and very popular with them all. He sang songs, and was hail-fellow-well-met, as we say, with all of them...."

Mr Pinson narrowly watched the face of Mr Lebaudy, and saw his eyebrows lift.

"... I think he must have been a student, perhaps a law student—I have a hazy recollection of something of the kind. Also I fancy, but I may be wrong, that there was some cloud or other about him at the end. They talked a good deal of him."

"Ah!" cried Mr Lebaudy. "We are there. I know. It was at the Brasserie Boucher! It was old Boucher who spoke. But you are wrong, monsieur. It is not on the left of the market. It is on the right, in a little ruelle off the Rue Chauveau-Lagarde. And I wonder—I wonder how an English visitor to Paris found himself in the Ruelle Michel talking about the Affaire Moreau! I wonder."

He looked closely at Pinson for a moment or two.

"Affaire Moreau?" said Pinson ingenuously. "What is that?"

"It was the sad business in the which——"

Mr Lebaudy suddenly checked himself.

"Well, never mind," said he. "I have not the pleasure of knowing monsieur. Do you reside in Westport?"

"Oh no," said Pinson. "In London. Merely here on a visit."

"Do you often go to Paris, monsieur?"

"Not often. From time to time."

"Ah well," said Mr Lebaudy, slipping off his stool and going to the door, "when you are in Paris again and visit the Ruelle Michel, tell my friend Boucher how glad I was to hear from him, and give him my most cordial salutations, won't you?"

It was a very obvious dismissal, and Mr Pinson took his leave with proper effusion of compliments.

VIII

At five o'clock Mr Pinson was seated at tea in the parlour of a dingy little house in a by-street of Westport, talking to Mr Joe Grainger.

His acquaintance with Mr Grainger was of long standing. Mr Grainger had been the superintendent of the detective service in the Westport police, and the grateful Home Office having allowed him to retire on a pension while he was in the fulness of his powers and enjoying the wisdom that came of twenty years' experience of the ways of the underworld, he had set up in a quiet way as a private inquiry agent. It was to Grainger that Pinson turned for help when he was involved in the Fallofield affair of which his wife and Elburton had spoken. They had a strong respect for each other—Grainger for the keen brain and the light heart of the lawyer, Pinson for the astuteness and the knowledge of the policeman.

Mr Pinson made the Colebroke case plain to Mr Grainger under pledge of absolute silence. He drew from his pocket his half sheet of note-paper and placed it on the table before him. With the help of the names upon it he told the story consecutively up to the point at which Mr Cobbledick's reminiscences left it. Then he asked,

"What do you make of it, Grainger?"

"First," said Grainger, "have any of the big bank-notes Mr Colebroke drew been traced?"

"What a question! Of course not. Elburton has been afraid to open his lips on the subject."

"Ah, that's a pity," said Grainger. "There might be a good clue there. What do I make of it?" He paused and tapped his fingers against his teacup. "Why, this: that for some reason or other, probably robbery, Mr Colebroke has been done away with. You will find that only the discovery of his body solves this mystery."

"I've thought of that, Grainger. I don't rule it out, but I can't bring myself to believe it. Argue with me," said Pinson.

"Well—why should he disappear and leave no trace? Wherever he is, he must know that his absence is causing great distress. If he is in love with this girl, for instance——"

"But, my dear Grainger. The girl is not distressed. She seems as happy as a summer day."

"Of course. She is relying on her father's word. But when the thing comes out, as it must, she will be distressed enough. Then, think of all the suspicious circumstances there are. The money. The row with the chauffeur Julep. He hangs about after his dismissal. When Colebroke disappears he disappears. Neither of them has been seen since. Look for Julep. That's the line, Mr

Pinson."

Mr Pinson showed him his note "Julep— Liverpool."

"Well, Grainger," said he, "I'm on another line. But you are right: this one can't be neglected. Will you follow it up? If Julep sailed for Canada about the time indicated, you will be able to pick up his tracks."

"Very well. I will. And may I ask what is your line?"

"I'm going to pursue an inquiry suggested to me by my friend Jean-Marie Lebaudy. Do you know Monsieur Lebaudy?"

"Quite well, but I should not have thought that convivial Froggy was a friend of yours, Mr Pinson."

"I never heard of him till Elburton mentioned his name at lunch-time today, Grainger, so you're right. I said 'friend' in a Pickwickian sense. Now, here's the train of ideas that took me to Lebaudy. One of the little ditties that Colebroke was fond of singing was a certain boulevard song about that haunt of pleasure the Chat Noir. Don't suppose you ever heard of it, but it's well known in Paris. When I was there some years ago it was a favourite song with the young sparks. I used to hear them roaring it in the cafés. Lebaudy, dealer in fruit and vegetables. What more natural than to think of the Marché St Honoré? The Marché St Honoré is surrounded by little streets abounding in little cafés. Friendship between Colebroke and Lebaudy. Must have been started in Paris. I experiment on Lebaudy. An hour ago I was talking to him in his office. I invented a café whose proprietor had given me a message of greeting for him. I couldn't remember the name. I drew a bow at a venture—I invented an Englishman who had been a frequenter of the café. You see, if Colebroke and Lebaudy became acquainted in Paris, ten to one it was in some such place. He took it like a lamb. Gave me the name of the café and the address and the owner's name, all in a casual conversation.

"I drew another, longer bow. I invented a cloud over the Englishman. At least I deduced the cloud from a thin train of argument, and I won't trouble you with it. Anyhow, the cloud was another good guess. Mr Lebaudy told me what it was—the

Affaire Moreau, though I have no more idea than your pipe what the Affaire Moreau was.

"And then, my dear Grainger, Mr Lebaudy suddenly shut up bang—like that! He smelt a rat. He practically showed me out. But I have all I want from Mr Lebaudy, and that's the line I'm going on."

"Extremely interesting," said Grainger. "A pretty piece of work, Mr Pinson. You always were a lovely cross-examiner. But I really can't see much to the purpose along that line. All this is at least two years old. What do you propose?"

"Exactly this, Grainger. There are two possibilities about Colebroke. One is that he is dead. The other that he is alive. I propose that you should assume him to be dead, look for his body, find how he died, and capture his murderer if he was murdered. I shall assume that he is alive, and look for the man himself. Are you content?"

"Absolutely. You've given me the chump end of the chop, Mr Pinson."

"Well, we shall see. One thing is essential: that until some certainty is in front of us, every inquiry must be absolutely confidential and Elburton's position must be respected."

Grainger saw that and agreed.

"Otherwise, a free hand?" he asked.

"Perfectly free," said Pinson. "I shall probably not see you for a week. Let us make an appointment. Shall we meet here at five o'clock in the afternoon this day week?"

"Five sharp," said Grainger.

IX

At six o'clock Mr Pinson picked up his chauffeur, Cobbledick. He bade him wait ten minutes, and went into the hotel to write the following letter:

MY DEAR ELBURTON,

I have some important business which calls me suddenly to London. I must be there tomorrow, Saturday. As Sunday is dies non for the professional affairs of a briefless barrister, I shall probably spend it with my wife and family. You may depend upon seeing me again on Monday evening at latest.

Will you, by the way, telegraph to my London address the date (year and month will do) at which W.C. returned from Paris? I should like to have this first thing in the morning.

Ever,
NOEL PINSON.

He entrusted this letter to Mr Cobbledick, explained that he was obliged to return by the express to London, and sent him home. He telegraphed to Mrs Pinson, caught the train at seven o'clock, dined on board, smoked a large quantity of cigarettes, cogitated during the rest of the evening, and was at Paddington at midnight and in his Adelphi flat before one.

"Just a flying visit," he told his sleepy wife. "I am going to Paris in the morning. Can't take you. You would be in the way, for I'm bound for places where they don't take married ladies, and I shall probably be there only a few hours. I don't want anybody to know I've gone."

And within a few minutes Mr Pinson was asleep.

At half-past two the following afternoon he landed at Le Bourget and taxied into Paris. He booked a room at the Hôtel Edouard Sept, which was conveniently near his goal, had a late luncheon, and walked out on to the Boulevard.

"At four o'clock in the afternoon on a Saturday," he said to himself, "Monsieur Boucher is not likely to be very busy. I will straightway go and talk to him."

He crossed the street, dived into a narrow by-way which led him to the market square of St Honoré, and so to the Rue Chauveau-Lagarde. He remembered the Rue Chauveau-Lagarde: in a dingy old house in that street that terrible personage the British APM had his office during the War, and Mr Pinson had cause to curse the waste of precious hours in that dingy old house during his one short leave in Paris. But he had never noticed the Passage Michel until now he looked intently for it.

Almost a tunnel between tall houses was the Passage Michel. The Brasserie Boucher was a tiny bar almost in the middle of it.

Mr Pinson pushed the swinging door and entered. The interior was even smaller than the signboard promised. It had a long counter with a zinc top, and just enough room for thirsty people to sit between it and the window. At present there were no customers.

A gentleman with a glossy black beard, almost the counterpart of Mr Lebaudy's, sat behind the bar reading a newspaper and smoking a cigarette. He looked up and seemed surprised to see Mr Pinson.

"Monsieur," said he, putting down his cigarette.

Mr Pinson politely raised his hat, which gesture was a further cause of astonishment, and asked for a bock.

The gentleman with the beard procured him a foaming drink in a long tumbler standing on a saucer.

"Phew!" said Mr Pinson. "It is very warm today."

"In town, yes," replied the gentleman with the beard. "Monsieur is detained in the region of the market this afternoon?"

Pinson looked intently at him.

"Well then," said he, "in fact I came in to inquire for Mr Boucher."

"Ah!" said the gentleman with the beard, which he wagged with satisfaction. "I said to myself when you entered, 'Papa Boucher, the English gentleman has called not merely to drink a bock on a hot afternoon. There is some other reason.'"

"So," said Mr Pinson, "I have the pleasure of speaking to Mr Boucher himself?" And he held his hand across the bar, while Mr Boucher shook it at length.

"Boucher, that's me," he replied.

"I am lucky today," Mr Pinson resumed. "I come to Paris. I bethink myself of a message given to me in England. I walk into the Passage Michel, I enter the Brasserie Boucher, and the first person I see is Mr Boucher himself. Extraordinary!"

In the course of which speech Mr Pinson seemed to work

himself up to a high pitch of enthusiasm, plying his smile and his ingratiating manner, and inducing commensurable enthusiasm in Mr Boucher too, though that gentleman could have no notion of what it all meant.

"A message for me—from England!" he exclaimed, with wonder.

"Ah yes. In England, in the town of Westport, I made the acquaintance of Mr Jean-Marie Lebaudy, and I happened to mention to him that I was going to Paris. He said to me, 'If you go to Paris be sure to call on my friend Boucher at the Brasserie Boucher in the Ruelle Michel, and give him my most cordial salutations. Thus, Mr Boucher, here I am."

Mr Boucher stretched his arm over the counter again for another handshake. But he also shook his head.

"Lebaudy—Lebaudy? I do not for the moment recall Mr Lebaudy. He went to England?"

"Ah, surely you recall Mr Lebaudy? He was in the vegetables and fruits. He went to England some years ago to commence business. How shall I remind you? Hold! I have it. He was here—he used to come in every day—at the time when everybody was discussing the Affaire Moreau."

"Affaire Moreau?" Mr Boucher echoed. "Ah, ah! We are there! It comes back to me. Lebaudy—certainly. He was in the vegetables and fruits, a *courtier*. I remember. The Affaire Moreau—of course! Lebaudy was a great friend of the Englishman Mr Caulbrouck. So, so! Lebaudy sends his salutations to Papa Boucher! I should not have thought it. No, the devil I shouldn't. Tell him, Monsieur, that I am greatly flattered. How it is strange—that the Affaire Moreau should unite us across the sea!"

Mr Pinson at this point pulled up a stool and sat on it close to the counter.

"What is more strange still," said he, "is that you should be acquainted with Mr Colebroke, who is a friend of mine."

"Tenez! You are a friend of Mr Caulbrouck! Là, là, là!"

Mr Boucher stretched his arm across the counter for a third handshake.

"I have not seen him for a long time. I suppose you do not know whether he is in Paris now?"

"If I know whether——"

Mr Boucher pulled up short and his bold brown eyes looked straight into Mr Pinson's.

"No, monsieur," said he. "I do not know whether Mr Caulbrouck is in Paris now. I have not seen him since years."

"Eh, well," said Mr Pinson, slipping off the stool, "I am delighted to have made your acquaintance, Mr Boucher, and I shall not forget to give your greetings to Mr Lebaudy when I get back to England."

He raised his hat and moved towards the door. "Au plaisir, monsieur," he said.

"Au revoir, Monsieur Pinson," said Mr Boucher.

X

Having completed his business at the Brasserie Boucher, Mr Pinson wasted no time. He went immediately to the office of the *Petit Parisien* and requested to be allowed to examine the file of the paper for the first half of the year 1919.

The bound volume was brought to him with many warnings against making cuttings from it and the information that any extracts he required could be supplied at a fee. But Mr Pinson assured the charming young lady who attended to him that he wanted nothing more than to confirm a date.

Having consulted the telegram from Elburton which gave him a date, he turned back the leaves methodically until he espied the heading "L'Affaire Moreau."

It covered a brief announcement that the Moreau affair was finished, the Assize Court of the Seine having on the previous day sentenced Antoine Moreau to two years' imprisonment and acquitted Miss Margaret Vincent of complicity.

Complicity in what?

Mr Pinson racked his brains for some recollections of the Moreau affair, but failed to find any. It was just after the War;

people were thinking of other things. Apparently the citizens of Paris were so bored with the Moreau affair that the paper did not think it worth while to recount the charge, but merely gave the sentences.

He turned back and found many more references to the case. But he had to put in two hours solid reading before he finished his inquiry, making an occasional note.

The Moreau case, it seemed, was a charge against Antoine of that name of conspiracy with unknown persons against the safety of a certain famous Minister, and a charge against Miss Vincent of aiding and abetting. A poor little plot of some futile secret society whose every movement was well known to the police.

Antoine Moreau had been a law student before the War. Like many soldiers, he nursed a grievance, half personal and half political. Mr Pinson, in his hurry, did not trouble to discover exactly what it was: M Moreau's grievances were of less importance at the moment than something else. He sped backward through the file, looking for a name.

At last he found it—the name of Monsieur Westmore Colebroke.

Monsieur Colebroke had been a witness in the Affaire Moreau. He was called for the prosecution—much against his will, he said. He had no interest in the case; but he was an acquaintance of the accused Antoine Moreau, whom he believed to be a perfectly harmless fanatic, while his *amie*, Miss Vincent, an English girl, seemed to have no criminal tendencies. He knew Antoine before the War, when they were law students together. He met him once during the War. He—Monsieur Colebroke—enlisted at the beginning of the fighting, but was soon given a commission and appointed a liaison officer on account of the accident that he knew French. Thus for a brief time he was in touch with Antoine Moreau's regiment and they recognised each other.

After the War, Monsieur Colebroke resumed his life in Paris. Then he met Antoine Moreau again, but only on one occasion. It was in a little cabaret—the Brasserie Boucher, near the Marché St Honoré. He had been accustomed to call there because he knew the proprietor, M Boucher. On a certain evening (he gave the date) Antoine Moreau came in and they said two words of greeting before Moreau passed on to an inner room, accompanied by a number of young men, all laughing and talking. That was all he knew, and he had never seen Moreau since until the day of his appearance in court.

Given in a cool and detached fashion, this evidence did not seem to amount to a great deal, but it aroused the accused to fury.

As Monsieur Colebroke left the stand, Moreau broke into an explosion of abuse.

"Traître! Scelerat! Crétin! Chien d'Anglais!"

His counsel at last succeeded in pacifying him. And so, Monsieur Colebroke disappeared out of the files of the *Petit Parisien*. It was a month later that he had returned to Westport.

Mr Pinson shut up the file and went into the street. He was an extremely observant man, as Miss Elburton had remarked. He observed, on leaving the newspaper office, that it did not matter whether he crossed the road or kept straight on, whether he went eastward along the Poissonière, or westward along the Capucines, or dodged down towards the river or up towards the Boulevard Haussmann, the same thing happened—the same gentleman of inconspicuous appearance, in a lounge suit and a felt hat, took the same interest in his doings and paid the same attention to his footsteps.

Now, as he had been in Paris only an hour or two, and had spoken to nobody except Mr Boucher, it was curious that he should be shadowed in this way. There was no mistake about it. To make perfectly certain, Mr Pinson hopped into a bus going westward and rode as far as the Place de la Concorde. The Felt Hat alighted from the bus immediately behind him. Its owner was interested in the same flower beds in the Tuileries Gardens. When Mr Pinson hailed a taxi and told the driver to get to the Etoile as fast as his machine would go, the Felt Hat bolted into another taxi which followed it.

Mr Pinson was by that time perfectly certain. Wherever he went in Paris the Felt Hat would be, and he tried to double it no longer.

He returned to the hotel, went to his room and locked himself in.

Plunged in the depths of a big chesterfield, Mr Pinson plunged also into the depths of a long reverie.

"You are right, Pinson," he told himself, "and Grainger is wrong. Mr Westmore Colebroke is alive and in good health, and probably within a mile or two of you at this minute. Mr Westmore Colebroke, to put it with vulgar brutality, is hiding away from something or somebody. He has plenty of money; ergo, plenty of friends. He can pay them to spy on you, Pinson. He has done so. They are spying. But how the mischief they got on your track so soon I can't make out.

"How? Boucher, of course. But who put Boucher wise? You were particularly careful, Pinson, not to mention your name to Papa Boucher. But Papa Boucher had it pat. How did Papa Boucher know it? Naturally, he had received a telegram from friend Lebaudy. A wily old bird, Papa Boucher. He acted his forgetfulness of Lebaudy with perfect conviction. He almost deceived you. But, Pinson, there's one thing Papa Boucher could not make out, and that was why you were after Colebroke and how much you knew of his whereabouts. Hence Felt Hat and an absurd waste of money on taxi-fares.

"What does Felt Hat want? He may make himself a nuisance. However, let us dine and see what happens."

Mr Pinson went out to dinner. He had brought no clothes with him, and did not care for sitting in state at a lonely table in the hotel restaurant. As he passed out of the lift and across the hall, he saw Felt Hat on guard near the telephone box. When he turned into the Boulevard, Felt Hat was behind him. When he took a seat among the crowd in the Café Americain, Felt Hat sat down near by and ordered his dinner.

When Mr Pinson was in the middle of his omelette, Felt Hat

suddenly got up and, leaving his chair against the table, went out of the room.

"Felt Hat has gone to the telephone," said Mr Pinson. "Now we are for it."

He swallowed the rest of his omelette with indecent haste, called up the waiter, was liberal to him, and fled. It was not very difficult. Felt Hat evidently rested under the delusion that he was invisible to a blunder-headed Englishman.

Mr Pinson stopped a taxi and was borne in three minutes to a quiet street he knew of where he dived into a theatrical perruquièr's and bought an admirable chevelure of curly black hair to which were attached an equally luxuriant moustache and beard. He also invested in a little black grease paint.

The taxi took him and his parcel to the hotel, and he immediately disappeared into his room, No. 101. Shortly after, there appeared in the lounge of the Edouard Sept a distinguished-looking man, rather tall and thin, apparently a Russian Prince or a Pianist, who lolled in a cane chair near the office window dandling a cigarette.

Felt Hat, rather flustered, came into the lounge accompanied by another man. They looked around and then advanced to the office. The Russian potentate stared idly at them while they went through a ritual of winks and nods with the clerk, closing with the transfer of a note from the front to the back of the counter.

"Le numero 101?" said the clerk. "Il est chez lui."

"C'est bien un anglais?" asked Felt Hat's companion.

"Sans doute," said the clerk.

"Amateurs—mere amateurs!" said the Russian potentate to himself.

The two men left the counter and took a seat near him, facing the lift. They talked with such animation, his companion expostulating and Felt Hat explaining. From snatches of the conversation which reached him, the Russian potentate gathered that they were greatly mystified by the proceedings of one Pinson, who had arrived in Paris long before he was expected and before they could obtain definite information about him.

Gradually they relapsed into silence, and sat watching the entrance to the lift.

At nine o'clock the Russian potentate, having smoked a large quantity of cigarettes, yawned and stretched himself, rose from his chair, strolled to the lift and ascended. He vanished into No. 101.

On Sunday morning Mr Pinson rose at 7.30, having slept like a log for nine hours, bathed at leisure, went down for rolls and coffee, had his suitcase put on a taxi and caught the boat train at 9 o'clock for Boulogne.

Felt Hat followed him to the Gare du Nord in another taxi and saw him off the premises. He was in London at six o'clock and dined *en famille*—that is to say with the only portion of his family available, being Mrs Pinson, as Miss Dora had already retired for the night.

XI

Keeping the promise made in his hasty note to Elburton, Mr Pinson arrived at Longbridge on Monday afternoon, and was in time to take tea with Miss Maud and her father.

He assured Elburton that he had found Mrs Pinson quite well and that Miss Pinson seemed to have grown even in two days; and he conversed about a variety of things without approaching the subject of Elburton's complication.

"I was looking forward to some music tonight," said he to the girl, "but after dinner I want your father to give me his opinion in a rather conundrumish case I'm engaged on. Won't mind if I keep him an hour?"

"Not a bit," said Maud. "I have an old woman or two to see: I'll save them up for the evening."

She was a splendid actress, thought Pinson. While dear old Elburton accepted for gospel all he was told, Miss Maud, he perceived, had no use for his plausible explanations or his puzzling cases. She sensed something in the wind. But how much?

He was not left long in doubt. After tea Elburton returned to his office to clear up his business for the day. Mr Pinson strolled into the garden and sat on the bench which had been the recipient of his confidences three days before.

Elburton was, once more, a priceless ass. He could not see far enough through a brick wall to prevent smashing his nose upon it. Mr Westmore Colebroke very likely had some perfectly good reason for disappearing, and he had confided it to Maud Elburton under the pledge of secrecy. She was evidently well aware that in everything he said about Colebroke her father was lying like a gasmeter, and if she was the girl Pinson thought, she had a pretty good idea of the mess he was in and the impossibility of extricating himself from it. But how far had she guessed what Mr Pinson's mission and his motives were?

As if to answer the unspoken question, Maud Elburton came round the path to where he was sitting and joined him on the bench. What a jolly afternoon it was for the garden, he remarked. She assented. It was very jolly. It made one want to sing, said Pinson. And he began to hum,

"Je cherche fortune
Autour du Chat Noir
Au claire de la lune...."

"Yes," said Maud. "It makes one want to sing. But why choose a song about Montmartre by moonlight to sing in an English garden on a sunshiny afternoon?"

"Oh, goddess of the grove!" said Pinson, "I sit reproved. It was a most inappropriate lyrical outburst. I suppose the reason was that it was the last song I heard. The last tune I heard often runs in my head for days."

"Mr Pinson," said the girl, "you do not always tell the truth. That's a rude thing to say, but you will appreciate my meaning."

Pinson smiled at her sententious earnestness. She was very

young, and very nice.

"In stating that truism, Miss Maud," he replied, "you are either leading me on to a general confession of my masculine weaknesses, or you have some ulterior motive. Men were deceivers ever!—true. But what particular prevarication of mine have you got in mind now?"

"None in particular," she said, "All the lot. Your very presence in this garden talking to me is a prevarication. Your visit to London was a pretence. Your conundrum to be discussed with father this evening in an invention."

She looked him frankly in the eyes as she coolly summed up his shortcomings, with no anger, but as one stating curious and interesting facts.

"Oh oh, Miss Maud!" cried Pinson, with an air of mock grievance. "My lucky star is gone behind a cloud. Nobody loves me today."

"Oh yes," she answered. "I like you very well. You are nice, and you are clever. But you are not so clever as you think you are."

"Admirably put," said Pinson. "But, Miss Maud, let us see for a moment exactly how foolish I am. Don't interrupt me while I give you my asinine interpretation of what is passing in your mind. We will suppose that Miss Maud Elburton soliloquises—thus: 'This man Pinson has come down here for the express purpose of interfering in an affair that does not concern him. It is a very delicate affair, and, if he is as clever as he pretends, he ought to be able to see that the best thing he can do is to leave it entirely alone.' How do I get on?" said Pinson, turning to her.

"Fairly well so far," said Miss Maud.

"Well, Miss Maud continues her soliloquy, 'No doubt my father asked him to come down to talk over this delicate affair. But be ought to have realised at once that my father had the wrong end of the stick, and that I, who know all about it, could have put him right at any moment if I had not been under a solemn pledge of secrecy on the subject, and that I would die rather than break it.' Now, how's that, Miss Maud?"

"As a statement of fact it is near enough," she returned, "but

———"

"But what?"

"But—never mind. Go on."

"Well, here is Miss Maud again: 'I came into this garden determined that this man Pinson should be persuaded, if possible, to abandon the inquiries he is making. They are stupid and futile inquiries, and can only lead to the stirring up of danger to a person whose safety I prize very highly.' How is that, Miss Maud?"

Her head was now bent upon her hands as she sat beside him. He saw a flushed cheek and he heard a little sob, and a tear ran down between her fingers.

"But—Miss Maud!" said Pinson, putting a hand on her shoulder. "This is not the real Miss Maud. She is an extraordinarily upstanding, plucky girl, of great discernment. She is in possession of a secret which is hard to keep, but she keeps it. She is very lonely, especially as she cannot take her father into her confidence. But she has borne her loneliness bravely—until this asinine lawyer from London comes butting in and upsetting her calculations . . . Ah, now she is herself again!"

Miss Maud had looked up, patted her eyes with a handkerchief, and held out her hand to Mr Pinson.

"I'm sorry," she said. "I withdraw what I said. But oh—can't you see that this secret must be respected? That it is dangerous to inquire or to make any fuss? Mr Pinson, I implore you to leave it alone!"

"Ah now," said Pinson, "you are doing my cleverness less than justice again. I came today specially to assure your father that all his apprehensions were unfounded, to put an end to the inquiry he wanted to set up, and to tell him that I would not pursue it any further."

"Oh, thank you, thank you!" cried Miss Maud, smiling to him.

"But there is one thing I should like to know if you don't mind telling me," said Pinson. "Have you had any word from Mr Colebroke definitely or indefinitely since he left?"

"None directly."

"Ah then, perhaps, under the pledge of secrecy, I can tell you something which will cheer you up. I was in Paris on Saturday. I have every reason to suppose that Mr Colebroke is quite fit and active, and has so far escaped his danger, that he has very sound friends, and is likely to remain safe."

"Oh!" Miss Maud exclaimed, grasping Pinson's hand. "You saw him—you saw him!"

"No," he replied. "I do not think I saw him—you must remember that I never met Mr Colebroke. But from many things that happened I deduced his nearness and his safety, and my deductions are generally rather clever, you know! Walk with me up and down the garden, so that we can see anybody approaching, and I'll tell you all about it."

Nobody approached. They paced the garden during half an hour, while Pinson described to the girl his journey to Paris and his doings there. Her step lightened and her spirits rose. She laughed delightedly at the episode of the Russian dignitary. As they entered the house, she said to him,

"Count Pinsonsky—I was very rude to you. I apologise. I think you are much cleverer than you seem."

When that night Pinson and Elburton sat together in the dining-room with their tobacco. Pinson related the story to his friend in much the same terms. Elburton's relief was very great,

"How can I thank you, Pinson?" he said, "You have taken such a burden off my mind that I feel years younger than I did last week. It has been terrible for me to live in the house with that innocent girl, acting a lie to her, and fearing all the time that she was going to be the chief victim of an awful tragedy."

Pinson smiled.

"My dear Elburton," he said. "Miss Maud has no ideas of the sort you fancied and there is no need to put them into her head. If I were you I should leave the Colebroke mystery alone. It will solve itself when Mr Colebroke decides, in his own good time, that there is no need for further mystery. Shall we dismiss the subject? I go home again tomorrow and resume the daily grind.

Your little problem has not been so exciting as I thought it would be."

And Pinson remained of that opinion until the following afternoon. At Paddington Station he turned suddenly to nod to an acquaintance who passed him, and saw Felt Hat dodging behind a luggage barrow.

PART 2 MR GRAINGER MAKES A DISCOVERY

I

Mr Joe Grainger had his own methods of tracing facts hidden from the generality of mankind.

Almost invariably, when a commission was entrusted to Mr Grainger, that gentleman disappeared from the face of the earth for the time and a variety of other gentlemen took his place. They wore clothes and adornments which had been kept in order for them by Mrs Grainger, so that when, after Mr Pinson's departure, Mr Grainger said to his wife, "I shall want the big bag and I don't know how long I shall be away," his lady knew exactly what to prepare for him.

Mr Grainger in his own person being very well known in Longbridge, and all over the district, he performed a metamorphosis before leaving his house.

One of his favourite characters was that of a chauffeur-handy-man, who might be in uniform or out of it, and could hang about in all sorts of places without arousing curiosity. So it was a soberly dressed chauffeur with a sober-looking gladstone-bag who left the suburbs of Westport within an hour of his interview with Mr Pinson and went to the central telephone exchange. He sent a note to the superintendent, who ordered that the visitor should be shown to his office.

"Merely a private inquiry," said Mr Grainger; "but I want it kept particularly private, so that is why I bothered you instead of putting in a call from home. Can you get me through to Liverpool without the intervention of the girls on the switchboard?"

The superintendent thought he could, and he did by having the Liverpool Exchange connected directly with his office. Mr Grainger got through to the Cunard Line.

First, the ships which sailed for Canada between certain dates. He was given their names.

Then, was there a passage booked on any one of those ships in the name of Julep? No Mr Julep had sailed from Liverpool in March.

Mr Grainger thanked the superintendent of telephones for his kindness, went to the railway station, and within half an hour alighted at Longbridge. In a by-street of the little town there was a public-house where a chauffeur awaiting an engagement might stay the night, so Mr Grainger was informed, and have a bedroom to himself. There he disposed his gladstone-bag. The rest of the evening he spent in the tap-room of the hotel.

To which between eight and nine o'clock resorted Mr Cobbledick, having cleaned up and bestowed his famous Ford in the garage, and ordered a pint of his proper refreshment, which was a mixture of beer and porter, taken in a large glass mug.

The other chauffeur who happened to be sitting in the tap-room was not only a very respectable-looking but a most abstemious man. He told Mr Cobbledick, when they had drifted into conversation, that so far from being a Pussyfoot or anything of that sort he liked to see other men enjoying their beer or their porter or their beer and porter together; but as for him, his silly head was so weak that even the mildest alcoholic beverages upset it, wherefore he drank only ginger-ale. But he was a slave to tobacco. Perhaps Mr Cobbledick would like to try a cigar?

Mr Cobbledick certainly would. He commiserated his companion earnestly upon the sore disability from which he suffered. Mr Cobbledick could imagine nothing more dreadful than being obliged to abstain from both beer and porter. However, he certainly liked the cigar, which showed that his companion had a pretty good notion of what a cigar ought to be, and led him on to reminiscences of the cigars with which customers had from time to time regaled him.

Yes, said the abstemious chauffeur, he was a stranger in Longbridge. He had only arrived that afternoon. He was to have met a prospective employer there, but he had received word that the gentleman must be absent for a few days—possibly a week or more. During that time he was to take lodgings and wait. So he had taken lodgings at the Plume of Feathers, and was now waiting.

"Ah," said Cobbledick, "that would be Mr Colebroke, no doubt?"

Yes, the chauffeur admitted, it would.

"A nice gentleman, Mr Colebroke—as nice a gentleman as ever breathed. And it was time he had a new chauffeur, for the last one he had was a stinkin' toad of a fellow if ever I should say such words. So you're a bit of a gardener as well as a chauffeur, no doubt. Your hands don't look it."

Mr Grainger regarded his well-kept hands and confessed that they didn't look it. But he hadn't been doing any gardening lately, and as for engine-dirt, well, it was wonderful what you could do with that grease dissolving stuff.

So it was, said Mr Cobbledick, examining his own huge and grimy fist, though he thought some people's hands must be more susceptible to cleanliness than others.

"What was the matter with Julep?" asked Mr Grainger. "Why was he fired?"

"Well, he and Mr Colebroke had a mortal row one day, and the next we heard was that Julep was going out to Canada. Everything was the matter with him. He was a down-looking, surly-tempered devil, and as mean—well, as mean as a dirty skunk could be."

Cobbledick took up his pint glass and measured its remaining contents with his eye. Mr Grainger invited him to exhaust them and then replenish the mug.

Half-way through the second pint Mr Grainger had discovered what was the matter with Julep. Though he was always willing to take a drink he never stood one. He borrowed matches and never gave them. He accepted cigarettes and never offered them. The cause of the row with Mr Colebroke was that Julep had been found selling stuff out of the garden, pocketing the money and saying nothing about it. And he, Cobbledick, would just as a matter of curiosity like to see Mr Colebroke's oil and petrol bills for the last few months. He would be quite prepared to learn that the little two-seater had drank more petrol and eaten more oil than a healthy sharrybang!

"However," said Grainger, "he's gone to Canada now, so I suppose that's the last we shall hear of Mr Julep."

Cobbledick supposed so. He pitied Canada if that was the case.

"Mr Colebroke been away some time?" asked Mr Grainger. "When did Julep leave? And did Mr Colebroke take the car with him?"

Mr Colebroke left soon after Julep got the sack, Cobbledick remembered, and had not been back since. He did not take the car with him, because it was still in the garage. Mr Colebroke had no garage at his house because there was no road to the garden at the back. He garaged it here in the hotel coachhouse, where the famous Ford resided. Julep hung about Longbridge some time after he had left Mr Colebroke's service. He was a sort of engine worshipper, and could not help messing about with a car. He was in the garage messing about with it on the very day Mr Colebroke was called away. Cobbledick remembered that night because he was in High Street on his way home between eleven and twelve when he saw Mr Colebroke letting himself in with his latchkey.

Cobbledick interrupted these reminiscences to clean up the remnants of his second pint, and yielded to the solicitations of Mr Grainger to have another. Of which the first mouthful lubricated his recollection if it did not assist his articulation.

Yes, he remembered it quite well because he had such a start that night. He had been having a few drinks in this very room, and after he had said goodnight to Julep he stood talking with some friends of his: they had an argument that lasted an hour. Then he was just turning off the High Street on the way to his humble dwelling and the society of Mrs Cobbledick, when he heard two tremendous back-fires. He thought indeed that it was a tyre burst and a smash, and somebody cried out. So, fearing a bad accident, he ran back to the street again. When he got there, nothing was to be seen, but he heard a car in the distance going away from him. It must have been somebody passing through to Westport who had been driving badly and got his charges firing back: there was such a lot of rotten driving these days.

"So there is," said Mr Grainger, sipping from his glass of ginger ale.

"You'm right," said Cobbledick, following suit from the pint glass. "Not but what that fellow Julep was one of the neatest drivers you could wish to see."

"Then I shall have to be on my p's and q's," said Mr Grainger. "Never seen anything of Julep since?"

"No. Not since that day. Well—I must be going—unless you'd like to have another gasattack?"

Mr Grainger smiled at this description of his favourite beverage, shook his head, and said "So long. No doubt I shall see you about now and then."

"Rather," said Cobbledick, and in a demonstration of maltous friendship shook hands with him. "You won't stay long at the Plume of Feathers, I s'pose? If you should want lodgings, there's the rooms Julep had at Mother Colwill's down South Street. She ain't got anybody else in yet."

"That's useful!" said Grainger. "What number in South Street?"

"I don't know as there's any number, but 'tis the next house to the garage doors—just round behind here."

"Thanks," said Grainger. "So long—good night."

II

His colloquy with Cobbledick had lasted till past nine, but Mr Grainger, having looked at his watch, decided that there was time to do a little more before the Plume of Feathers received him for the night. Having allowed his boon companion time to get clear, he sauntered out and found South Street, running at right angles to High Street immediately next to the hotel. The little house indicated by Cobbledick adjoined the wall of the inn-yard.

Mr Grainger knocked upon the door.

"Mrs Colwill?" he inquired of the old lady who answered. She owned the name.

She had been recommended to him, Mr Grainger explained, as a possible landlady. He had been engaged as chauffeur-gardener to Mr Colebroke, and was awaiting his return. If he could have the rooms recently occupied by Mr Julep he would be glad. He apologised for calling so late, but he had arrived only that evening and put up at the Plume of Feathers. He was anxious to get settled as soon as possible.

To all this Mrs Colwill nodded her head. She invited Mr Grainger to enter, and half an hour later Mr Grainger was still sitting in her kitchen, engaging Mrs Colwill in an entertaining conversation. That is to say, Mr Grainger listened hard while Mrs Colwill talked. From time to time he expressed the fear that he was wasting her time with his idle gossip, but she assured him that it was a pleasure to listen to him and went on again.

Mr Grainger found it difficult to keep the old lady on the rails he wished to travel, which went in only two directions, for she shunted off in a dozen others at every point. But, as he was to succeed to the condition and to the rooms of Mr Julep, it was fairly easy to come back to that subject at intervals.

So that in the course of time Mr Grainger discovered, as he expected, additional and very curious facts about Mr Julep. He was naturally most interested in what happened to Mr Julep at the end of his career in Longbridge. He heard with patience Mrs Colwill's version of the row with Mr Colebroke, which appeared to have been not so much the cause of Julep's departure as a circumstance connected with it. Mr Colebroke was very angry with Julep, and had said some nasty things about him; but he had not left immediately. His scheme of emigration to Canada had been on the cards for some time. What seemed to Mrs Colwill so strange was that at the end he should go off so suddenly as he did.

"I don't mind telling you, Mr——"

"Mr Wilson," said Grainger, promptly.

"I don't mind telling you, Mr Wilson, that I was greatly astonished—I was literally staggered. Now, wouldn't you have been astonished and staggered yourself if you had a lodger (supposing such a thing to be possible) and your lodger paid you up to his last week, then came back and asked to stay a few days longer, and then—hey presto! he vanished and doesn't even take his things away with him?"

Mr Grainger had no doubt he would have been both staggered and astonished.

"What!" he cried. "Didn't take his things? And they are still here? I can't believe it, Mrs Colwill."

The idea that anybody should doubt her word caused Mrs Colwill to bridle. She lit her bedroom candle and rose majestically.

"If you doubt my word, Mr Wilson, come with me and you shall see for yourself."

Mr Grainger accepted the invitation with remarkable alacrity, and she led the way upstairs. Mr Julep seemed to have been well accommodated, for he had two excellent rooms on the first floor. In the sitting room there were no evidences of his occupation. In the bedroom, however, clothes were neatly folded in a wardrobe.

"Mr Julep's clothes," said Mrs Colwill, as who should proudly produce evidence for a disputed word. She pointed to a wooden trunk.

"Mr Julep's trunk," she said, "with more of Mr Julep's clothes." But her real triumph was to come. She produced a key and unlocked a cash box that stood on the dressing table.

"Mr Julep's money!" she cried, raising a packet of Treasury Notes and jingling some loose silver. Mr Julep's money, which he asked me to keep for him in my cash box until he was leaving."

"Very astonishing. Very staggering!" remarked Mr Grainger.

"How much is it?"

"Twenty-four pounds thirteen and sixpence to a penny," said Mrs Colwill. "And there it is, and there it remains until Mr Julep calls to reclaim it."

"He must have been a warm man to have been able to leave so much money behind and not notice it," said Mr Grainger.

"A saving man, I should say. A very frugal man, Mr Wilson. He always paid me to the minute—not a penny more or less. A very honest man, but, if I should say so"—and she took a look at Grainger which made him smile—"if I should say so, a little near, so to speak. No little compliments, you understand me, at Christmas or any festive season. But there, of course, that's nothing to make a song about."

Downstairs again, Mr Grainger fished for the exact date and time when Mrs Colwill last saw the elusive Mr Julep. She was as confident on that point as on all the others.

"At half-past ten o'clock or thereabouts in the evening of the 18th of March he said he was going to have a look at the car, to make sure that the gears were locked—I suppose that is sense, though I don't know what it means. He went out for that purpose, and he never came back again. I haven't seen him since."

The old lady was so evidently gratified by the sensational impression she was making on Mr Grainger that he acted staggered astonishment and encouraged her confidential mood to the nth degree.

There was one more line upon which he was anxious for her to follow him. It was a little delicate, but he induced her to walk there by a roundabout way. The pleasant smallness of Longbridge, its neighbourliness, its attractions, the beauty of the district, which he had observed from the train, the fact that everybody seemed to know everybody. Mr Grainger supposed that strangers did not make their appearance in Longbridge once in a blue moon. Apart from the trippers from Westport (whom she held in severe despite), Mrs Colwill thought strangers were very few. The town did not grow; it was not often that a house became empty, and then there was much competition for it. The only thing was that occasionally somebody went off for a holiday and let his house furnished for a month or two.

Mr Grainger perked up.

"I shouldn't have thought there were many houses of that sort in Longbridge, from a casual look at it," he said.

No, not many, Mrs Colwill agreed. But after all Longbridge was quite a nice town for people bent on holiday, and anybody who could get a house like Mrs Pethybridge's, with a view over the river, must have a very enjoyable time—though what foreigners could see in walling themselves up in a place like that and never going outside the door, she could not imagine.

"Foreigners?" Mr Grainger asked, with an interrogatory eyebrow up. "I should hardly have thought there were any foreigners in such a very English little place."

Mrs Colwill apologised. She didn't hold with foreigners herself, but they were certainly foreigners who had taken Mrs Pethybridge's house for six months. Hardly anybody ever saw them, but the tradesmen who called knew they were foreigners: at any rate, neither they nor their servants could talk plain English.

And then Mr Grainger, looking at his watch, discovered that it was nearly eleven o'clock, and took a hurried leave, arranging to bring his bag along next day and occupy the rooms vacated by Mr Julep.

III

There was a third episode to come of Mr Grainger's first night in Longbridge.

He apologised to the landlady of the Plume of Feathers for his late return. He said he had no doubt the whole household had to be up bright and early in the morning; he would not trouble about any refreshment but go straight to his room.

There he drew the blind close, locked the door, and opened the big bag which Mrs Grainger had packed for him. He rumpled up his pyjamas and threw them on the back of the chair—turned back the bedclothes and pulled them about. He punched the pillow. He poured water into the basin and washed his hands. He cleaned his teeth and left the water in the glass and the toothbrush on the washstand. He threw the towels on the floor.

In ten minutes Mr Grainger's neat country bedroom looked as if a very disorderly person had overslept himself in it and risen in a great hurry.

Mr Grainger then turned again to the bag and extracted:

A pair of rubber shoes
A pair of rubber gloves
An electric torch
A jemmy
A roll of some dark substance—

all of which, except the shoes, he bestowed in his pockets. Mr Grainger then took off his boots and assumed the shoes. Next he found in the bag a little box which contained a pencil and some colours, and spent a few minutes before his mirror so converting the features of Mr Grainger that he could easily have mistaken himself for another person. Finally, he put his boots in the bag, locked it up, switched off the light, and sat in darkness for the space of twenty minutes.

The house of Mrs Pethybridge of Longbridge lay on the outskirts of the town, overlooking the river just where it broadened into the estuary at whose seaward end was Westport. It was a substantial villa of Victorian origin, surrounded by small ornamental grounds, heavily treed, which for border a six-foot wall and thick hedges of laurel and escalonia.

In front of the house stretched a lawn, which had been well kept but now was somewhat dishevelled. A pleasant lawn, for at the river edge there were two or three big cedars which cast a deep shadow and gave shelter from the sun to some garden seats looking down the estuary to the West.

On this particular night one of the cedars stood in direct

line of a bright beam of light which shone from a window —apparently the dining-room window, and there was a patch of blackest shadow immediately behind its noble trunk. Consequently, the person who stood there could not be seen by anybody two yards away. He stood motionless with the greatest patience while the shadows of people moving inside the room passed across the curtains; while the distant chime of a clock sounded a quarter to twelve, and twelve o'clock; while the figures ceased to move and the light went out; while the chime gave out the quarter-past and two lights appeared in upper windows; while the clock said half-past and the lights were extinguished, leaving the lawn in perfect darkness, and the roofline of the house dimly showing against a starlit sky; and while the clock said a quarter to one.

Then suddenly the person who had stood behind the cedar was no longer there. Moving as silently as a gnat flies through the air, he was under the wall of the house. He listened at a door, at a window, at another door, at a pantry window, at every aperture in that house on all its four sides. He returned to the window from which the light had shone.

Invisible, silent, he took from his pocket an instrument with which he described a circle about six inches in diameter on the middle pane of the window. Then he took a roll of black stuff and, detaching the end, held it against the pane and smoothed the roll down over the circle. It adhered to the glass.

He listened acutely. There was no sound but the little distant murmur of the water. He waited...

At the first note of the chime which preceded one o'clock, he pushed his hand hard upon the black stuff. It gave without a sound that could be heard against the chiming of the bells. He pulled at the black stuff, and a circle of glass came away with it.

His hand went through the aperture. The window was presently raised. He was in the room. He looked back through the window into the garden. It seemed not to be overlooked from any direction.

A beam of light flashed round the room in less than a second and vanished. It was long enough to show him that the room had only one door, and the way to it. He stole invisibly and silently across to it.

He passed it.

Still as the grave he waited. No sound: no glint of light. Another flash from the electric torch lit up for a second the corridor in which he stood. He took no notice of doors or of the stairway at the end of the corridor. His glance passed quickly round the cornice, searching for something.

It was there—in a corner by a hat rack. At the side of the hat rack was a chair. The silent figure passed in the darkness to the chair and mounted it. He unfastened the glass door of a little box affixed to the wall. A dozen movements of agile fingers inside rubber gloves and all the fuses in that box hung loose.

The electric lighting system of Mrs Pethybridge's villa was out of action.

The silent, noiseless figure moved back to the doorway through which he had entered the corridor, and having passed into the dining-room, locked the door. At the window there was a vague oblong of faint light. He stole across and, turning his back to the window, switched on his torch again and examined the room in more detail.

One piece of furniture in it alone interested him. It was a desk standing in a recess. Keeping the light under his coat so that it concentrated in one direction, and did not show near the window, he went to the alcove, drew up a chair and sat in front of the desk. One of those heavy structures of mahogany with a revolving cover. He tried several of the keys on his liberal bunch. None would fit. But it was a trivial task to pick the lock with a little hook, to hold back the spring for a moment and roll the cover over. He glanced at pigeon holes, opened drawers, quietly, quickly. In three minutes he had been through the contents of them all and selected a loose packet of half a dozen letters apparently at random, for he did not take them out of their envelopes. He slipped them into his pocket, closed the desk, placed the chair where it had stood, switched off his light, and waited to allow his eyes to become accustomed to the darkness and find the faint oblong of the window.

He stepped to the door, unlocked it, and was passing towards the window when he heard a woman's voice. It seemed to ring very loud in the stillness, though it was not raised high.

"Victor!" it said.

At the same moment there was the sound of knocking at a door, and then a man's voice growled a reply.

The silent figure reached the window, raised it enough to allow him to pass through, closed it, put his hand through the circular hole and latched it. He listened.

The two voices were audible, but he could distinguish nothing of their words. Picking up his piece of black stuff, he almost detached the circle of glass from it, found his tube of mucilage, anointed the edge of the circle and deftly fixed it in the aperture.

Keeping close to the walls, he moved to the other side of the house and listened. The conversation seemed to be proceeding in a bedroom over a verandah that stretched the whole length of that wall. The silent man had evidently made up his mind to overhear it. He tested the strength of the verandah posts, but found them too shaky to climb without noise. Therefore he strained his hearing to a high pitch of attention, standing as close as possible under the window of the room.

The talk was of the failure of the electric light. The woman's voice spoke perfect English; the man's a mixture of English with a foreign accent and French.

"Ça ne fait rien," he said. "You are too nervous, mignonne.'

"But it is very strange, Victor, and I'm sure I heard something."

"Hallucinations, imaginations," said he. "The light fails to function; you are nervous; you think you hear."

"I can't help it. Ever since—I've been afraid. You do not tell me. You conceal something."

"Rien du tout! I conceal nothing at all. I have told you a hundred times, there is nothing to fear. Now, mignonne, go away and sleep."

"Victor! you do not understand England and English law. It is different. It works quietly and finds out things—slowly, but it is very sure."

"No doubt, your English law is very clever—merveilleux! Who denies it? But there is nothing for it to find out, mignonne. Now, go away. Tu as des alumettes? Non? Voilà—here is a box. Light yourself back. Good night. Dors bien...."

A gleam of light issued from the window. The silent man squeezed up to the wall, stole round again to the lawn, and so away.

IV

Mr Grainger was almost as bright and early next morning as any of the inhabitants of the Plume of Feathers. He came down as soon as he heard movement, ate his breakfast, paid his bills, took his bag off to Mrs Colwill's and assumed possession of the apartments which had been Julep's.

He spent the whole day in the snug sitting-room. Mrs Colwill entering to ascertain whether and when he would like food, found him with the table covered with papers, busily writing. Entering again three hours later, she observed that he was still engaged with pen and paper. If she thought it strange that a chauffeur should devote so much time and labour to literary work, she said nothing about it.

By the time Mrs Colwill at his request brought him strong tea and a miniature mountain of bread and butter, Mr Grainger had completed his task. He had before him a pile of manuscript in his own handwriting. Drinking tea and munching bread, he considered it.

The bulk of it consisted of laborious translations of letters addressed from Paris to M Victor Leduc at The Cedars, Longbridge, Devon. They were allusive letters, and Mr Grainger, being without the key of the allusions, could not make much of them. They seemed to be chiefly concerned with the activities of a political group, which he judged to be small and of no great consequence. They made no reference which could remotely attach to the business in Mr Grainger's hands, and contained no explanation of Mr Leduc's presence in England and in Longbridge. If his political game was a dangerous one (which appeared to be quite possible) then very likely he was in sanctuary against the attentions of the Paris police.

Mr Grainger turned the letters down and came to the conclusion that the time and ingenuity he had spent on a very neat little burglary were wasted. It was Mr Pinson's suggestion which had thrown him off the scent. But he was not going to be led further astray.

The Julep trail was the trail to follow. What Mr Julep did and where he went on the night of Colebroke's disappearance after he had left this room at ten o'clock, that was what Mr Grainger wanted to find out.

He turned up the remainder of the papers.

Unknown to Mrs Colwill, the literary-minded chauffeur in the intervals between her visits had made a very thorough investigation of Mr Julep's apartments and his belongings. There was not a pocket of Mr Julep he had not turned out, and not a corner of box or bag he had not examined.

Before him on the table lay the two crucial things he had found. He took up the first and re-read it:

16th March.

DEAR JULEP,

I am very sorry in a way that I cannot listen to your application to be taken back. You are an excellent driver and a capital gardener, and in those capacities I have no complaint to make of you.

If I had not detected you in a piece of flagrant misconduct I should not want to part with you.

You may affirm that I am mistaken as often as you like, and I shall not believe it unless I have corroboration of what you say, and there is no likelihood of that. Although I did not see you there, I am as certain as a man can be of anything that you were in my office on Tuesday night under the most suspicious circumstances and overheard a private conversation. You denied it, and the denial was, I believe, a lie.

That is all I can give you as answer to your request, unless you bring by tomorrow evidence that will convince me I am wrong. In that case I will make you ample amends.

Yours truly,
W. COLEBROKE.

Having re-read this letter, Mr Grainger sat for several minutes in deep contemplation. Then he turned to the second:

114A Manchester Road,
Shepherd's Bush,
20th March.
MY DEAR OLD CHARLIE,
Thanks for your letter of the 18th. What luck! I wish I knew a guy or two like that. Of course, I will take care of the boodle. Anyhow, when are you going to come up and let me help you spend some of it? It sounds like a fairy tale. You aren't pulling my leg, are you?

Certainly I'll keep the paper safe, though I can't make head or tail of it.

A month or two ago you were doddering about going to Canada. Now you are drivelling about going away indefinitely but hoping to see me soon. What does it mean?

Heaps of love. Ever your
BELLA.

And having re-read this letter, Mr Grainger sank into deeper contemplation than before. It afforded him much food for reflection, though he could ill spare the time for it, because Mr Julep had never seen this letter. Mr Grainger's were the first eyes that had lit upon it since it was written and sealed. It had evidently reached the lodgings after Mr Julep's final departure. Mrs Colwill had stood it on the mantelpiece in front of the clock, awaiting his return. Mr Grainger had damped the envelope and waited for it to soften before he took the letter out. He had substituted a sheet of plain paper, fastened it and restored it to its place on the mantelpiece.

Mr Grainger, although he did not betray any flurry, was in desperate haste. There were three things to be done urgently, the last of which was a call at No. 114A Manchester Road, Shepherd's Bush. And Shepherd's Bush was a great way from Longbridge.

The first of these things could not wait. Mr Grainger locked up his papers in the big gladstone-bag, made a neat packet of letters which he tied up with string, took his hat and went forth. In the street he dropped the packet of letters and they happened to fall in the only muddy place in all South Street. With an expression of disgust Mr Grainger retrieved them, cleaned them as best he could by banging them against the wall, and walked on.

The maid at The Cedars, Mrs Pethybridge's house down by the bridge, answered a ring at the door and saw a chauffeur standing there.

"Is Mr Leduc at home?" asked the chauffeur.

"What name, please?" said the girl, in a foreign accent.

"Oh, Mr Leduc would not know my name. Tell him I have a private communication to make to him. I'm not cadging; I don't want a situation. I merely want to hand him something that will interest him, my dear."

Mr Grainger doubted whether she understood half his harangue, she looked so blank. He amended it in his best French, which was not very good, but good enough for her to comprehend.

"Mistaire Leduc is not at home," she said.

"Mrs Leduc, then," said Grainger.

"Madame is also . . ."

Mr Grainger did not give her time to complete the perjury. Seeing a movement at the end of the hall behind her, he raised his voice.

"Dear me!" he cried. "What a pity. It was so important that they should have these letters. Still, if they are not at home there's nothing to be done, is there?"

"Will you leave the letters?" asked the maid.

"Oh no," said Mr Grainger, "I can't do that. I must give them into the hands of Mr or Mrs Leduc. Most unfortunate——"

And as he had bawled these remarks at the top of his voice, he was not surprised when a lady appeared in the doorway and the maid gave place to her. She was a youngish woman, not thirty, he thought, and might have been English.

"What do you want?" she said. "Berthe, you can go in and leave me to deal with this man."

Mr Grainger touched his hat.

"Pardon, ma'am," said he. "I wished to see Mr Leduc."

"Mr Leduc is out," she answered. "I am Mrs Leduc. What is it you want?"

"That's a pity," said Mr Grainger. "I wanted to make a personal communication to him."

"Well, you can't make it now. Mr Leduc has gone to Westport and won't be home till late. You can see him if you will call in the morning at half-past nine."

Mr Grainger was looking very boldly in her eyes—or rather boldly for a manservant—and watching every play of her features. He decided that she was telling the truth.

"Unfortunately, ma'am, I shall not be able to call in the morning. I had better give you the communication. It is that I picked up this packet of letters just now in the road outside."

Mr Grainger continued to study her face while he spoke and pulled the letters out of his pocket. She betrayed no surprise, curiosity or relief—no emotion of any sort. She took the packet from him and turned back two or three of the envelopes.

"Thank you," she said. "It looks as if Mr Leduc dropped them out of his pocket by accident. Were they tied up like this?"

"No, ma'am. They were loose when I saw them. I just put a bit of string round to keep them secure in case I should not be able to see him today. It never occurred to me that he might have dropped them . . ." Mr Grainger looked steadily in her face. "I somehow or other got the idea that they might have been stolen," he said.

"Stolen!" Her surprise at the suggestion was quite genuine.

"A funny idea—stealing letters like that. No, my man, I should think Mr Leduc must have dropped them. Anyhow, I am much obliged to you for returning them."

"Oh, that's nothing," said Mr Grainger. "Good evening, ma'am."

"Won't you let me give you something for your trouble?" she asked.

"Of course not, ma'am. No trouble at all." And Mr Grainger was already on his way down the drive.

Nothing in this, he said to himself. They had evidently not even discovered that somebody had broken into the house. They attached no importance to the letters. If they had inquired why all their fuses were disarranged in the middle of the night, they had taken no trouble to understand the explanation. He had at first connected these people with Mr Pinson's clue; but there was nothing in it. The trail of Julep was the thing. He would get on the trail of Julep.

V

But there remained one other thing to do in Longbridge before he could apply himself to the search for Mr Julep. He eagerly wanted to be at No. 114A Manchester Road, Shepherd's Bush; but there was no time to do this one other thing and catch the evening train.

He would have to drop the idea of reaching Shepherd's Bush tonight and trust to circumstances for his next step.

The urgent thing was to get inside Mr Westmore Colebroke's house and establish relations with his housekeeper, Mrs Paddon. Mr Grainger did not doubt that he could succeed in this, but it would take a little time. There was first the need for documentary evidence of his *bona fides*.

He returned to his lodgings, and this time he locked himself in his sitting-room. He turned out the original of Mr Colebroke's letter to Julep and studied its handwriting. He produced from that Pandora-bag which Mrs Grainger had prepared, for him an assortment of stationery. It was a peculiarity of Mr Grainger that he kept an assortment of other people's letter-headings. He collected them. He had letter-headings of the Royal Hotel, Westport, of several London hotels, and of one or two private offices. But he rejected all these and ran through his stock till he came to what he sought—a card with the crest of the Westport Club embossed on it.

With Mr Colebroke's letter before him, Mr Grainger sat down and painfully wrote two or three sentences on the card, which he placed in an envelope and addressed to himself at the Royal Hotel, Westport, "to be called for."

At seven o'clock, he rang at the door opposite the Market Hall, and was answered by the neat maid.

No, she told him, Mr Colebroke was not at home. Expected tonight? She was sure she couldn't say. Perhaps he had better see Mrs Paddon, the housekeeper. Mr Grainger indicated what pleasure it would give him to see her, and when that lady appeared presently in the passage he removed his chauffeur's cap with the greatest respect.

"Good evening, ma'am," he said. "I'm the new chauffeur. Ordered to report tonight."

"Goodness gracious!" exclaimed Mrs Paddon, starting back a step or two. "What are you talking about?"

"Beg pardon, ma'am. I said I'm the new chauffeur. Mr Colebroke ordered me to report tonight."

"Mr Colebroke! But—when for mercy's sake did you see Mr Colebroke?"

"Oh, I haven't seen him at all," said Mr Grainger. "I understand he's been away for some time. But I have a letter from him. I was recommended to him by my old employer, who is a friend of his at the Westport Club, and he took me on the testimonial. He couldn't see me, as he was going away. Here is the letter, if you'd be good enough to look at it, ma'am."

And Mr Grainger produced his envelope and extracted the card from it. Mrs Paddon took it to the doorway, held it in the light and read in Mr Colebroke's neat handwriting:

The Westport Club.
18th March.
MR WILSON,

Please report at my address for duty on Saturday evening the 24th June. I expect to return by then. If I am not back, run over the car carefully and tidy up in the garden. Ask Mrs Paddon to let you look in the right-hand drawer of my table. It is full of papers relating to the car, and you will find Julep's list of necessary renewals among them. Get at this immediately.

W. COLEBROKE.

"Goodness gracious!" she exclaimed, handing the card back to him. "So you're called Wilson? It's very strange——"

"What's very strange, ma'am?" asked Grainger.

"About Mr Colebroke appointing today and never letting me ——" She checked herself. "However, that's no business of yours. Better come and find the papers at once. Where are you staying?"

"I've taken the rooms that the other man had," he replied, following her through the passage and up the stairs, and into the room with the three windows overlooking the street.

Arrived there, Mr Grainger paid not the slightest attention to Mrs Paddon's proceedings. He was burning into his mind a picture of the room, and a geometrical picture, a picture with measurements. The summer evening sunshine flooded it. filtering between the slats of the Venetian blinds. It was a perfectly open room, not a screen, not a curtain, every corner visible.

Mr Grainger was trying to guess the solution of a riddle. Where in a room like this could a man be concealed to listen to a private conversation? Where? Not under the table. There was but a kneehole. No piece of furniture in that place was big enough to hide a man.

But on the evening of Tuesday March 15th Julep was in that room unseen and eavesdropping. Where?

Mrs Paddon had been pulling for a few moments at the drawer

on the right hand side of Mr Colebroke's table.

"It's locked," she said. "Or I can't get it open. Will you try?"

Then Grainger, as if he had suddenly bethought himself, cried out,

"Oh of course. Now I see. I couldn't make it out before. Here's a message scribbled on the envelop. 'Third key on ring in Toms's desk.'"

He showed it to her.

"Botheration!" said Mrs Paddon.

"I'm sorry to give you so much trouble, ma'am," said Mr Grainger humbly. "Perhaps it can wait till Mr Colebroke comes back."

"Oh no, indeed," Mrs Paddon rapped out. "If Mr Colebroke gave the instruction it must be carried out. Wait here, and I will find the key."

"Shall I come with you, ma'am?" asked Mr Grainger.

"No, of course not. Whatever for? Wait here."

When she had left the room, Mr Grainger breathed a great sigh of relief. He pushed the door close and settled to rapid calculation and equally rapid work.

As Mrs Paddon would certainly find no ring of keys in Mr Toms's desk and would certainly search the office for it, Mr Grainger reckoned that he would have five minutes to himself at least. Here in this room, he felt convinced, was the secret he sought.

One minute for calculation. What was it that he found strange about this lawyer's office? There were law books; there was plain and handsome furniture, a glass-topped table in the newest style, with drawers and a kneehole between. But it was singularly bare for an office. Where did Mr Colebroke keep his books and papers, his documents, his valuables? There was not even a safe.

A safe! That was the thing that Mr Grainger missed.

Four minutes left. He went to the door and looked along the landing. The wall of the room was of the ordinary sort. No safe in that. At the fireplace end no room for a safe. On the side of the three windows—nothing: they were cut in the exterior wall of the building.

Then Mr Grainger turned his attention to the panelled end of the room where the elder Colebroke's portrait hung. He looked carefully over it. A nice piece of panelling, comparatively modern, he should say, and in excellent condition. It had only one flaw—a little hole near the corner away from the windows, about half way between floor and ceiling.

Mr Grainger looked at the edges of the hole and felt it. The aperture was not large enough to poke a finger into. Mr Grainger whipped out the hook which had served him the night before and probed the hole with it. And presently he pulled out a piece of metal.

It was lead. He fingered it, looked at it closely. It was a flattened bullet of very small calibre. Why flattened? Why not through that panelling into the brick or plaster behind?

Mr Grainger probed the hole again. His hook struck neither wood nor brick nor stone, but metal.

His minutes were flying. But Mr Grainger had the key to the secret now.

Indeed, it was no secret at all. He pushed sideways against each section of the panel in turn till one slid back, revealing a small cavity in which was the lever handle of a safe. The wood panels simply covered its steelwork in order that the symmetry of the walls might not be disturbed.

Of course this could not be opened without the combination, which was probably in the sole knowledge of Mr Colebroke himself.

Mr Grainger idly handled the lever. He staggered back as the wall seemed to come towards him. A long iron door was opening on its hinges. It came back slowly. Mr Grainger gasped. He heard the footsteps of Mrs Paddon on the stairs, quickly swung the concealed door home. He noticed that as it closed the panel slid back into place. He stepped to the table and leant upon it.

He was a very cool and experienced policeman, but Mr Grainger's knees were trembling as Mrs Paddon fussed in.

"I can't find any keys, Wilson," she said. "Mr Colebroke must have made a mistake."

"Never mind, ma'am——"

"What a peculiar smell!" cried Mrs Paddon, interrupting him. "Do you notice anything?"

"No, ma'am. Nothing. But I have a bit of a cold in my head, ma'am." Grainger sniffed and imperceptibly edged her towards the door. "No, ma'am, nothing at all. Well, I'll be going. I can look over the car and report on Monday. Perhaps Mr Colebroke will be back himself by that time."

He talked Mrs Paddon down into the hall and took his leave.

The first thing Mr Grainger did was to go to the taproom of the hotel and swallow two glasses of ginger-ale and light a strong cigar. He was pale and he had not recovered from that shivery feeling in the knees.

VI

His momentary vision behind the oak panel of Mr Westmore Colebroke's office had staggered Mr Grainger a great deal more than Mrs Colwill's revelations, and when he reached that lady's house he was in a state of physical weakness and great confusion of mind.

The one thing that Mr Grainger now desired more than another was to be able to speak with Mr Pinson, and he knew that was impossible, for Mr Pinson had gone off to Paris on a wild-goose chase and Heaven knew when he would be back.

From the first Mr Grainger had been certain that Mr Pinson was wrong in his theory; and now he had the most convincing evidence of that error. Yet he could not move without Pinson. There was no knowing where such a discovery might lead, whom it would affect, how it would react on several people.

There was Mr Elburton, who had been responsible for putting about the story of Colebroke's temporary absence on business. How would it affect him?

There was Miss Elburton, who appeared to be deep in love with

Colebroke. One could imagine how it would affect her.

There was Pinson himself, who had engaged Mr Grainger to do this work: to him the report was due, and to nobody else. Mr Grainger knew what would happen immediately he said a word to anybody of the discovery he had made in Colebroke's office. He decided that for the present the discovery should remain a secret. There was only one other person in the world beside himself who knew of it. He would find that person.

That such a secret should exist in a place that must be known to many people, should have existed for months and never have been suspected!—it was, as Mrs Colwill would say, "staggering." If the strong-room had been locked, even . . . But no doubt all who knew of the strong-room—the servants, for example—supposed that it had been locked up by Colebroke before his departure. There was, in fact, no reason why it should have been suspected, since nobody knew there was anything to suspect.

Except one man. And Mr Grainger would find that man.

The strong-room would doubtless continue to hide its secret until Mr Grainger chose that it should be revealed. As for that which the strong room contained—no delays that Mr Grainger could impose upon it would matter in the least, for it had reached the Great Infinity.

Having reflected to this effect, Mr Grainger recovered from the shock he had received and set about planning his action for the immediate future. He had slept little the previous night. He was tired to the point of exhaustion. It would be just possible to catch the midnight train at Westport and reach London early in the morning. But after all, a secret which had kept so long would keep one day more while Mr Grainger recuperated in the comfortable bed that had belonged to Mr Julep.

And then Mr Grainger unaccountably had a sudden aversion from occupying a bed that had been slept in by Mr Julep. The distaste grew as he contemplated the idea.

The issue was that Mr Grainger called upon Mrs Colwill to give him a little supper and announced that he would be going to Westport for the night. He would like to pay for a week's lodgings in advance, and he would return on Monday. Mrs Colwill, apparently suspecting some designs upon the cash-box which contained Mr Julep's fortune, surreptitiously removed it from the bedroom to her own apartments, a motion which Mr Grainger noticed with a smile. Then she procured him his supper, and, after writing a letter, Mr Grainger took his gladstone-bag and his departure.

Mrs Grainger was not surprised to see him when he reached the little suburban house in Westport at about eleven o'clock. He came and went with the utmost irregularity and irresponsibility, and Mrs Grainger was always prepared to make up a large or a small bag for him as occasion required. If he had wanted a pemmicanised kit for a journey to the North Pole, she would have prepared it without any other comment than a warning not to catch cold. This time, however, he wanted a small bag for London, and that quickly, while he changed the clothes he was wearing and transformed himself from a chauffeur into Mr Joe Grainger, a respectable middle-class citizen well and favourably known to the police.

His last injunction to Mrs Grainger before he left to catch the midnight train was: "If you do not get a postcard from me by Tuesday morning, post this letter to Mr Pinson and telephone to Scotland Yard this message." He scribbled on a sheet: "Mr Grainger asked me to 'phone you." "They will know what to do," said Mr Grainger.

In a sleeper on the train he sank easily into that slumber which he was sure he would not have secured if he had tried for it in the bed where Mr Julep had slept.

VII

Mrs Pinson and the Honourable Dora had expected their lord and master at tea that Tuesday afternoon. He had said he would be with them, and he had never disappointed them before. But he did not appear at half-past five as arranged, nor did he keep his regular appointment to romp with the Honourable Dora before she went to bed, nor to dine with Mrs Pinson, nor to play the gramophone to her after dinner.

The evening in the flat in the Adelphi was extremely tame and boring. Mrs Pinson sat wondering why he had failed not only to arrive but also to let her know why.

Being a meticulous man, Mr Pinson would certainly have done one or other of these two things except for *force majeure*. While Mrs Pinson sat wondering, Mr Pinson was also wondering, and wondering very hard indeed.

The wonderment began when, in the afternoon, he arrived at Paddington Station and saw Felt Hat dodge behind a luggage barrow. There was a great crush on the arrival platform, and a strong competition for taxis. Not enough of them could stream down the incline from Bishop's Road to satisfy the demand. Mr Pinson was therefore rather lucky to get hold of a porter willing to attend to his wants alone, who went off and by some magic got hold of a taxi on whose step he rode up to the place on the platform where Mr Pinson stood. Having expressed his gratitude for the attention in silver tones, Mr Pinson put his suitcase on the seat, got in, gave his address in the Adelphi, and was soon whizzing along Praed Street and up the Edgware Road.

He felt quite sure that he had given Felt Hat the slip this time, because it was next door to impossible for him to have obtained a cab in time to follow. It was more than a little absurd, this shadowing, especially as the chase was over, and he was about to dismiss the affair of Mr Westmore Colebroke from his mind and settle down again to the prose of his chambers in the Temple and the poetry of his flat in the Adelphi.

When he reached Piccadilly Circus, there was a block. The roads were up, and a tremendous swirl of slow-moving traffic was being directed by perspiring policemen.

Seizing an opportunity, his driver turned into Shaftesbury Avenue instead of going across with the stream to St James's Street, and was presently squirming through narrow side streets in Soho, in the apparent effort to find a way round.

Mr Pinson had not taken very particular notice of the route he followed, and had not observed that he had gone north instead of south of the Avenue; nor had he remarked the street in which the brakes of the taxi were suddenly applied as it turned sharp into a yard whose doors were banged behind it.

Almost as the doors banged Mr Pinson was getting out of the cab. But he was a moment too late—a mere moment. As his foot poised for the descent he was pushed back into the cab, with a wet swob over mouth and eyes, and held down on the seat for a minute or two, at the end of which Mr Noel Pinson was a limp body bent back half on the floor and half on the cushions, as neatly and expeditiously doped as ever a patient could wish to be.

When Mr Pinson came to his senses again he was alone in a room. He awoke with a splitting headache and an almost resistless desire to be sick. It reminded him of a muddy CCS in Flanders. He felt exactly like this when he came to after the gentleman in the white coat had taken a piece of 5.2 out of his leg. Slowly he realised that the occasion was a very different one. There was nothing whatever the matter with his leg. Only his dignity had been wounded.

Then Mr Pinson, who greatly admired neatness, thinking it over, admitted that this was a very neat job which he would never have believed anybody could perform in the West End of London at five o'clock on a June afternoon.

He had been too cocksure. When he saw Felt Hat at Paddington he ought to have been on his guard. When he obtained a taxi with such mysterious ease while the earls and belted knights and (for all he knew) the dukes who tumbled out of the Cornish Limited Express could hardly get a taxi for love or money. And especially he ought to have been on his guard when his driver failed to follow the obvious route from Piccadilly Circus to the Strand.

Also, he had been too contemptuous of the whole business. He had expected no such sequel to his visit to Paris, and having dismissed Westmore Colebroke from his own mind, he thought erroneously that other people had equally lost interest in him.

Which, clearly, they had not done. Felt Hat and his friends strongly resented Mr Pinson's intrusion into their affairs. And the next thing for Mr Pinson to do was to ascertain what those affairs were, in order to extricate himself from this undignified position and relieve the natural anxiety of Mrs Pinson and the Honourable Dora.

The room upon which he looked round with bleary eyes was lit by one window, and it was to the window that Mr Pinson first directed his attention. Through it he saw a blank wall at a distance of ten feet. Below him was a lane leading into a stable yard, quite silent and disused. He was three storeys high. There was not another window in sight. No view over the roofs to any landmark he could recognise. He was somewhere in London, for the noise of traffic reached him as a waving sound, rising and falling. His window faced west, for the sky above the blank wall was very bright. He looked at his watch. It was half-past six o'clock.

Mr Pinson turned to the door. A good door—and, of course, securely locked. Mr Pinson was a prisoner.

But he was not condemned to penal servitude or even to hard labour. A complete inventory of the room showed him that he was to be in an easy division. It contained a bed, fresh-made; toilet necessaries; a couch on which he had been lying when he awoke; a table laid with a passable dinner of cold viands, fruit, and a bottle of wine. In the absence of cheerful conversation over his meal, he could have entertaining reading: the evening papers were stacked on a chair!

Mr Pinson smiled, and the smile developed into a laugh.

He had been vaguely considering which of two courses he should take—run amok, batter the door, smash the glass of the window and endeavour to draw the attention of the British public to him (he even thought for a rapid moment of a rope made from the bedclothes and a descent to the yard below); or stay where he was, watch events, and pick up what crumbs of knowledge he could from his captors when they should deign to make their appearance.

On the whole, he decided, the more comfortable and the more amusing way would be to take the latter course. He thought that, clever as his unknown friends were, he could easily be their equal at bluff, and he promised himself some excellent entertainment when their scheme developed.

Thus it was that Mr Pinson laughed as he sat down at the table and ate his dinner, found the wine passable, lit a cigarette, and read the evening papers.

Not until an hour had passed was his peace in any sort disturbed.

Then the key turned in the door and a gentleman entered with a knock and the exclamation "Pardon!"

"Not at all," said Mr Pinson. "Come in."

He recognised the gentleman. It was the same whose conversation with Felt Hat had been overheard by a Russian count, or a pianist or something, in the hall of the Hôtel Edouard Sept.

"I 'ope," said the gentleman, speaking English with some diffidence, "that you have well dined."

"Excellently," said Mr Pinson. "I can't thank you sufficiently for your lavish hospitality. Exquisitely considerate of you, seeing that I was a poor man, not only to pay my taxi but to provide me with a banquet worthy of Heliogabalus. Will you smoke, m'sieur?"

Mr Pinson held out his cigarette-case. His visitor took a cigarette and Mr Pinson lit it for him.

"The one thing wanting," said he, "was coffee. But of course I admit that in England we do not know how to make coffee. Therefore, we give the coffee a miss. If there were another glass, now, I would suggest to you that this wine——"

"I have dined," said the gentleman. "If you wish coffee——"

"Oh no," Mr Pinson replied, "far from it. I am now quite satisfied. I shall take the greatest pleasure in an hour or so of conversation, and then to bed. How long am I to understand this generous invitation lasts? Is it a formal stay of some duration, or only a long weekend?"

The gentleman did not answer for a moment or two. He sat looking at the smoke curling off the end of his cigarette.

"You English," said he at last, "are curious, very droll. You have an idea most extraordinary of the blague."

"Ah yes," said Mr Pinson, who was blowing smoke rings to the ceiling. "I have noticed the same thing. The English for delicate irony, and the French for rare old practical jokes. But what would you have, monsieur? The nations cannot be all alike."

"You English," the gentleman repeated, "have a droll of an idea about the blague. But you also have much of what you call common-sense."

"That is a great compliment, monsieur. I will try to live up to it," said Mr Pinson.

"You English, too," said the gentleman, "have a very high sense of honour."

"These," said Mr Pinson airily, "are general sentiments very flattering to my patriotic vanity. I will try, directly, to think out something equally nice to say about the French nation."

"There is no necessity, Mr Pinson," the gentleman remarked.

"Ah, there," said Mr Pinson, "you have the advantage of me. I have not yet had the honour of knowing your name."

"It does not matter. Call me Mr Laroche. I am nobody. But Mr Pinson is another affair. Mr Pinson is a well-known advocate of the English bar. He is proud of his common-sense. He is, without doubt, anxious to return to Madame Pinson and his family. Mr Pinson is an honourable man. If he finds himself mistaken he will admit it. If he pledges his word he will keep it."

"Monsieur Laroche," said Mr Pinson, with a deprecating gesture, "you are too kind. You credit me with all the virtues. Nevertheless, as you say, if I find myself mistaken, I will always admit it. Am I mistaken in supposing, for example, that this excellent wine is a notable brand of the Vin de Vouvray? It seems to me to recall sunny days in the enchanting valley of the Loire. I think of Joachim du Bellay as I drink it. I want to sing with him of 'la douceur angevine.' No doubt you admire as much as I do his famous verses—

"'Plus me plait le sejour qu'ont batis mes aieux
Que des palais——'"

"Ah, Mr Pinson," said Mr Laroche, "another day it would be most interesting to discuss with you the poetry of Joachim du Bellay. But at the moment, one has not the time: it is a pity."

"Oh, pardon me," cried Mr Pinson. "I had no idea you were in a hurry, Monsieur Laroche. As for me, I have nothing particular to do this evening, and, as I nurse a mania for French poetry, I should have liked to exchange quotations and opinions with you. Especially about the modern boulevard ballad. Do you recall that most fashionable lyric:

"'Je cherche fortune,
du Chat Noir'?

But I forget again. You are pressed for time. Don't on any account let me detain you."

"I will not," said Mr Laroche. "And I am very anxious not to detain you."

"Not at all," Mr Pinson replied. "I assure you that, even if you detain me without worrying about it, I am enjoying myself enormously."

"But you would without doubt be better pleased if you were permitted to return at once to Madame Pinson."

"Ah, my dear sir," said Mr Pinson, "there you touch me on a tender spot. As between friends, now, is it fair to place me in this dilemma? You force me to choose between my domestic joys and the delights of your hospitality! Now, in my opinion, both have their proper place in the scheme of things, and should not be brought into rivalry. Even the most domesticated man must make a night of it sometimes. And why not tonight?"

VIII

Mr Laroche discarded his cigarette-end and rose. Standing in front of Mr Pinson's chair, with his hands resting on the table, he spoke earnestly.

"Mr Pinson," he said, "I beg you to be serious a few minutes. This affair is very disgusting to me. No, that is not the word. What is it you say?—ah, distasteful. This affair is very distasteful to me."

"To me, on the contrary," said Mr Pinson, "it is entirely delightful. I am simply revelling in it."

"You seem to be a kind man—as we should say, sympathetic. Why do you amuse yourself with the troubles of other people?"

Mr Pinson very deliberately selected a new cigarette and lit it from the stub of his old one.

"Monsieur Laroche," he said, looking him steadily in the eye, "you misjudge me sadly. I am a most humane person. But you accuse me of trifling with the woes of other people! Why—how can that be? I return from a visit to the country. I find myself at Paddington Station. You offer me your hospitality—in a somewhat unconventional way, I confess—and I accept it. I have a most delectable dinner, and now I have the pleasure of your company over my cigarette. That is all I am conscious of doing since five o'clock this afternoon. Now—where is the torture? And whose feelings am I outraging?"

Mr Laroche had listened to Mr Pinson's diatribe with manifest impatience.

"You carry your drollery to excess, Mr Pinson," he answered. "You know very well what is the reason of our action. We know very well what is the purpose of yours. We see that you are in the error—you are mistaken. We wish to show you the proof of it if you will promise to do no more."

Mr Pinson shook his head.

"With an overwhelming desire to be polite, my dear Monsieur Laroche, I haven't the ghost of a notion of what you are talking about!"

"I am talking about your inquiries in Paris and elsewhere."

"Paris! Ah yes, I did spend a weekend in Paris. I love Paris next to Touraine and Anjou. Don't you think Paris is exquisite in June? But—inquiries? What inquiries?"

"At Boucher's. At the *Petit Parisien*. Perhaps elsewhere."

"Ah, Boucher! He is at the brasserie near the Marché St Honoré. Why—my dear Mr Laroche, so far from making any inquiries at Boucher's, I went there to deliver to him a message from an old friend."

"Yes, I know, Mr Pinson. The friend was Lebaudy to whom you went to deliver a message from Boucher, and you had never in your life seen Boucher. The idea was clever, but not clever enough. You see, I know all about you."

"Then perhaps you will tell me why I was making inquiries and what they were—for I haven't an idea myself what you are driving at."

"It is not necessary to fence any more, Mr Pinson. You were making inquiries about certain activities of certain people, and you were making them on behalf of Antoine Moreau. And I tell you we will not tolerate any interference from Moreau or from anybody on his behalf. And I tell you we will not hesitate to stop interference. You have evidence of that. You are a prisoner here, and we will keep you a prisoner unless we get your word of honour that the interference shall cease. You are an Englishman of honour. I will take your word, and that is sufficient."

Mr Pinson was silent. He betrayed none of the astonishment he felt. He continued to puff his cigarette. At last he said,

"May I ask what is the edge you have on Monsieur Moreau?"

Mr Laroche looked puzzled.

"Ah, that is slang," said Pinson. "I beg your pardon. Why are you at enmity with Monsieur Moreau?"

"You ask that!" Mr Laroche exclaimed. "He has, no doubt, deceived you. The League was at the very point of success when he came out of prison. We welcomed him, as no doubt he has told you. But his mind was—what? There is an English word for it—something to do with ships. Ah, yes—his mind was warped by a desire, overwhelming, for private revenge. He seeks only one thing—to injure an old friend of himself and a very dear friend of mine. He has no doubt failed to tell you all the truth: he has got you by false pretensions—hein? You, an

English gentleman, would not be working for a scoundrel—not willingly, eh?"

"Certainly not," said Mr Pinson.

"Then you give your word of honour to leave it all alone, to do nothing more—and we say adieu. You return to Madame Pinson, and we go away to Paris, quite sure of the honour of an English gentleman."

Mr Pinson noted the expression of relief which the countenance of Mr Laroche had assumed.

"Not so fast, my dear sir," he said. "I could certainly give all the undertakings you require. But I should not like to let you down by doing so. You are not aware of it, but you have got hold of the wrong man. I know nothing whatever about any of the matters you mentioned. The League—for example. What League? I didn't know there was a League."

Mr Laroche seemed surprised. He receded a step or two.

"And though," Mr Pinson continued, "I cannot say I didn't know there was a Monsieur Moreau, I can truly say that I never saw him in my life, never had any communication with him, and certainly do not represent him in any way whatever."

The surprise in Mr Laroche's face became bewildered astonishment.

"You are an English gentleman." he said, stressing on the fact as if it were his sheet-anchor, "and you could not deliberately lie to me, I think. But you have been at Longbridge and you have been at Westport. You played one trick on Lebaudy and another on Boucher. Yet you say you have not been in touch with Antoine Moreau. It is curious, very curious." Mr Laroche looked Mr Pinson in the eyes, and he returned the gaze. "Would you tell me why it was you were at Longbridge and in Paris, chez Lebaudy and chez Boucher? If not Moreau, what was it?"

"That," said Mr Pinson, "is a secret, and it is not my secret. I cannot tell you. Nor can I say that it may not possibly be linked up with Moreau and the League in some remote way. But I have no interest in Moreau. I feel rather hostile to him. And as for your League, whatever it is, I detest politics—wouldn't touch it with a ten-foot pole. But tell me why you associate Longbridge and Mr Moreau?"

"Assuredly you cannot ignore the fact that Moreau is at Longbridge, Mr Pinson?"

"Good gracious!"

Mr Pinson jumped out of his chair. He hesitated a moment as if calculating.

"Moreau at Longbridge? Indeed I was ignorant of the fact, and it may be of the greatest importance to me. Since when? Since how long has Moreau been at Longbridge?"

Mr Pinson asked the question with some excitement.

"Since a few weeks after his release from prison, which was in the beginning of the year, I do not remember the exact date."

"Good heavens!" cried Mr Pinson. "The very time!"

"Which time?" Mr Laroche asked.

"Ah, that's a part of the secret I mentioned," said Mr Pinson. "Will you——"

"Zut!" said Mr Laroche, holding up his hand. "What is that?"

A noise of loud voices in altercation had suddenly burst out below stairs. Mr Laroche went to the door and listened.

"Legall!" he shouted down. "Quel vacarme! Qu'est-ce que c'est?"

The reply was muffled, and an English voice rose clearly.

"That'll do now, if you don't want all Scotland Yard on you. Stand back and let me pass."

A smile passed over Mr Pinson's face. He touched Mr Laroche on the arm.

"A friend of mine, I hear," said he. "Will you leave this matter to me? On parole, you know, Monsieur Laroche."

That gentleman bowed and stood aside. Mr Pinson went out to the landing and called,

"Grainger! Did I hear your voice? Will you come up this way? I want to introduce you to a friend."

With a tremendous rumpus of stumbling on the stairs, Mr Grainger presently appeared, dragging after him Felt Hat. He had his fingers twisted in Felt Hat's collar and his knuckles in

Felt Hut's throat, and Felt Hat was almost blue in the face from suffocation as Mr Grainger flung him into the room.

"Ah, there you are, Mr Pinson!" said he. "I tracked 'em down with a little help—and a lot of luck. I've got Mr Taxi-driver safely looked up downstairs, and here are the other two. Now, what about it?"

"A little misunderstanding, I fear, Grainger. First let me introduce you to my friend Mr Laroche. Mr Laroche: Mr Grainger, a very good friend of mine. I suppose you thought I was missing, Grainger? But I simply came in to dinner with Mr Laroche: who, I think, is going to be very useful to us in the business in hand."

Mr Grainger had stood in the doorway with amazement in his eyes as Mr Pinson spoke.

"Well, I'm——" he began.

"Not at all," said Mr Pinson. "You are not damned, Grainger. You are only mistaken. Mistakes will occur in the best regulated careers. How did you get here? But first I will apologise to Monsieur over there for your mistake. Accept our sincerest apologies and regrets, monsieur," he said to Felt Hat, who was nursing his neck in a corner of the room.

"I've been looking for you for two days," said Grainger. "Mrs Pinson told me you had gone down to Westport and were returning by the Limited. I was at Paddington. In the crowd I missed you till it was too late. I just saw that damned taxi go off. I followed, thinking you would be driving to the Adelphi. And then you didn't come. It's taken Scotland Yard till now to trace that cab."

"Phew!" Mr Pinson whistled. "Scotland Yard! Is any of it downstairs now?"

"Only one man on guard outside the mews, but others within call."

"My dear Grainger," said Mr Pinson, "oblige me by sending them off and releasing the taxi-man. Tell them everything's OK. We don't want them in this."

"All right," said Mr Grainger, "I'll send them away now. But we shall soon want them right enough. Mr Pinson, I've found him!

And my theory was right, and yours was wrong."

"What!"

Mr Pinson staggered and turned pale.

"I say I've found him—or what is left of him. And I'm running a great risk by delay in making it known. But I took the risk till I could tell you. You gave me the chump end of the chop, as I said."

PART 3 ADVENTURES OF MR PINSON

I

"So that was how he was killed!"

Mr Pinson and Mr Grainger were seated in the train which left Paddington at ten o'clock. "I seem to be living at Paddington Station," Mr Pinson had remarked as he got out of the cab to begin his second journey of two hundred miles that day.

Grainger had given him an account of the happenings at Longbridge during his absence up to the point of his visit to Mrs Paddon and his discovery of the strong-room.

"It is quite clear," said Pinson, "that I should never make a detective. I noticed the difference in the length of the two rooms, but I had not observed the absence of a safe, and a strong-room never occurred to me: it is so old-fashioned in a small house."

"Yes," said Grainger, "it is a bit out of date, Mr Pinson. But, to do you justice, I should never have thought of it either if I had not known of the existence of two such rooms in Westport. One was at a wine merchants', where the old boys used to keep their very special brands, and the other was at a lawyer's office. I had only a minute to look, but this was just such another place, built in massive stonework with a great iron door."

"And he was shot! So that was how he was killed! . . . Wait a moment, Grainger. Let me take it all in."

Mr Pinson sat back in his corner and closed his eyes.

"I can't see it all, Grainger. You just tell me how you see it all.

Begin at the beginning."

Mr Grainger was a methodical man. He took from his pocket a little notebook in which he had made entries in skeleton.

"Very well, Mr Pinson," said he. "Here is my theory of the crime...

"For some reason not yet apparent, Mr Westmore Colebroke wanted on the 18th of March a large sum of money in cash. I don't worry about the reason. He wanted it. The 18th of March is a week off Quarter Day, and people often want money about then. It may have been a gambling speculation, a debt—really I don't think it is material to the case——"

"I hadn't thought of Quarter Day," said Mr Pinson. "But go on."

"He obtained that large sum of money in notes on the 18th of March, before the bank closed in the afternoon at three o'clock. He took it away with him to his office. I have no doubt he locked it up in his strong-room for use on the following day. You based your supposition that he had disappeared voluntarily on the fact that he had paid up all his accounts and cleared up his business. I draw your attention to the fact that it was the end of the Quarter. Mr Colebroke was a punctilious sort of man, and I have ascertained that it was his invariable custom to pay sharp at Quarter Day. The clearing up of his legal business was, I am convinced, a coincidence. There is no evidence to be got of any special arrangements to close it up. You must remember that Mr Colebroke's chief business was advocacy. He made his reputation in the courts as a pleader; and just at that time there was not much doing. At the Quarter Sessions which took place the next week the Recorder was presented with a pair of white gloves: the police courts had sent no business to him."

"H'm—h'm," said Mr Pinson. "Go on."

"The man Julep had been hanging around for a purpose after his discharge for telling Mr Colebroke a lie. What was his purpose? I don't believe in his affection for a motor-car. That's rubbish. His purpose was revenge, and revenge by way of robbery. He meant to commit a robbery on that very night. I will draw your attention to the fact that his letter to the woman

Bella, in which he told her of the good fortune that had come to him, was written on the 18th, and her answer to it was received after Julep had gone. Julep never saw it.

"I have no doubt that when Mr Colebroke reached home after bidding the Elburtons good night on the 18th, he visited his office on his way to bed. If he had not done so, he would be alive now. I don't suppose for a moment that Julep intended to murder him. Julep had been drinking in the hotel taproom till ten. At half-past ten, or it may have been later, he left his lodgings on the pretence that he was going to look at the car. But of course he never went near the car. He sneaked into Mr Colebroke's house—somehow. I think he had discovered that there was a large sum of money on the premises—possibly he knew there would be. He had overheard a private conversation some days before, which very likely was about the money."

Pinson nodded. "Yes—I see. Well, go on, Grainger."

"I'm pretty much in the dark, you know, Mr Pinson—because your instructions don't permit me to make open inquiries—as to who visited Mr Colebroke on the evening of the 15th of March, for example. Well, when Mr Colebroke entered the house and ascended the stairs, Julep was in his office. He could not get out. He hid in the strong-room."

"Oh, I say, Grainger," exclaimed Mr Pinson, "that's coming it a big strong! How the devil could he get in there?"

"The best proof," said Grainger quietly, "is that he had been there before. He was concealed there when he overheard the private conversation. There was no other place where he could have been concealed. I examined the office very carefully. Apart from the strong-room you could hardly conceal a cat in it."

"Even if that were so, once Colebroke had discovered him there he would certainly have altered the combination—especially as you suggest that he had put more than three thousand pounds in cash there for security."

"No, sir, nothing of the sort," said Mr Grainger. "He did not alter the combination because there was no combination! It is a very old place. It is fastened by a peculiar lever-bolt hid behind the panelling. The door opened almost as soon as I touched it. The security of that place is its secrecy—nothing else. Of course, having cleared out Julep, and not knowing but what he was off to Canada, Mr Colebroke never thought of him again."

"M-m," said Mr Pinson. "Well, continue. Julep goes in there to hide. And then . . ."

"And then, Mr Colebroke would have escaped if he had not himself gone to the strong-room. He did go. When he opened it, he switched on the electric light. Mr Pinson—that light has been burning ever since, and is now for all I know!"

"Ye gods, how ghastly!" cried Pinson.

"He switched the light on. I take it that Julep was crouching in a corner, or perhaps immediately behind the door, and as Mr Colebroke passed in he sprang out into the office. Even then, if there had not been a telephone on the table, he might not have been a murderer. But the first thing Mr Colebroke would do when he was surprised would be to come back after him into the office and challenge him, knowing that he had three thousand pounds upon him. It was then that Julep whipped out his gun. He became a murderer from that moment. There was nothing to do but to kill Mr Colebroke and take his chance of getting away.

"As Mr Colebroke advanced, he aimed at him, and Mr Colebroke stepped back. Julep fired once and missed him, and the bullet hit the wood panel. Immediately he fired again, and Mr Colebroke fell in the doorway of the strong-room. Julep instantly pushed him right in. His legs are doubled up against the door.

"Julep closed the door and escaped by the way he had come. There are many ways. I could get into that place without a tool of any kind. That's how I figure it out, Mr Pinson."

Mr Pinson sat silent for a while as the train roared westward through the night.

"A wonderful reconstruction, Grainger." He broke the silence. "If anything, it is almost too complete. Some things puzzle me. But we will leave them on one side. Except this: two shots at so late an hour in the quiet town of Longbridge must have made a deuce of a row. How was it nobody heard them? Where was Mrs

Paddon and where was the buxom maid? They must be heavy sleepers."

"Yes: it puzzled me. But somebody did hear the shots," said Grainger. "Cobbledick the taxi-driver heard them. He was attracted to the High Street by two back-fires, and he heard a car going away in the distance. I give him the car—nothing unusual in that—but not the back-fires. Anybody else who heard probably thought the same thing."

Pinson took the back of a letter and made a note.

"Yes," he said, "that's interesting. Well, Mr Julep has three months' start, eh? What about the fair Bella? No doubt she was what brought you to London."

"Oh, I've got Bella fixed all right now," said Grainger. "But she gave me some trouble. Or at least London did. What a place! Do you know Shepherd's Bush, Mr Pinson?"

"Only as an omnibus route and as the seat of the White City. I can't say I am equal to Shepherd's Bush. What about it?"

"Well, when I got to Paddington on Sunday morning, I went down on the Metropolitan to Shepherd's Bush Station and asked for Manchester Road. A policeman was able to direct me along some dirty by-ways under a railway viaduct, and I found Manchester Road—a terrible little place of mean houses. Of course, Bella had left Manchester Road. She would. People always do in London. But I managed to find out her family name, which is Waters, and her next address. She had left that too. So the only way was to go to Scotland Yard about it. They found her for me down in Camberwell. But it took them all day yesterday, and I didn't see her till this morning.

"Well, as you may guess, Mr Pinson, Miss Bella Waters, after having heard nothing of Julep for three months, has turned her affections in another direction. The magnet is a greengrocer in Camberwell.

"So she had heard nothing from Julep in three months!" Mr Pinson mused.

"Nothing," said Grainger. "And a very good reason why. Julep dared not go back to his lodgings—afraid to be seen where he was known; and he thought afterwards, when it was too late, of the letter she had probably written to him. If there were any inquirers that would put them on the track of Bella and of Mr Julep. Depend on it he was out of the country in less than a week. Think what devil's own luck he had! Mr Elburton's folly in giving a false account of the disappearance. What murderer could expect such luck? The absence of any effort to trace the bank-notes, too. And then, silence for three months! It's preposterous luck."

"It is, Grainger. The father of lies has been a good parent to Mr Julep. But what about Bella? I'm waiting to know about the document she had received to keep for Julep."

"Oh," said Grainger. "Here it is—one more nail in Mr Julep's coffin if we are lucky enough to find him."

He drew from his pocket a letter.

"I had to be very cautious with Bella, of course. I could not tell her why I was interested in Julep. I made up a yarn on the spur of the moment, when I saw her attitude towards him, which was indifference and perhaps a little resentment. I said that Julep was in difficulties and wanted both the paper and the money, but that if I could deliver the paper to him he would probably not worry about the money."

"What money?" asked Mr Pinson.

"It was a blind dash—a kind of inspiration. You remember there was something about money in her letter to Julep. I dived at it. If Julep had sent her any of the money, whatever it was, I was on velvet. If not, she could only deny it. Well, she had had money right enough, though she did deny it; for she handed over the paper like a lamb."

He handed the letter to Mr Pinson.

"The letter's the thing," said he. "But read it to me, Grainger. I like to have things read to me. I grasp them better."

Grainger read.

"DEAR W,

"Just a word of warning. M has been released from prison, and is swearing vengeance on you. He is dangerous. I daresay you could buy him off for 50,000f if you liked! If you don't, take care of yourself. Tout à vous.

"J.L.

"How do I get on with my English?"

"Ah!" Mr Pinson exclaimed. "That explains it."

Mr Grainger looked up.

"Yes," said he, "it explains it as clear as daylight. Julep thought he had got hold of a letter on which he could blackmail Mr Colebroke at his leisure, and he sent it to the woman for safe keeping."

"That's not what I meant, Grainger. But you're quite right. Evidently, the words 'prison' and 'buy him off' suggested profitable blackmail in the future to our ingenious friend. So you've fixed Bella?"

"Well, I've asked a friend at the Yard to have an eye kept on her movements so that we can lay a hand upon her at any moment when she's wanted. And she'll be a most important witness, Mr Pinson."

"She will be if your Julep theory proves sound, Grainger."

"Why!" cried Grainger in an injured tone, "don't you think it's sound? What's the matter with it?"

Mr Pinson soothed him.

"My dear Grainger, I didn't say there was anything the matter with it. I said 'if.' Of course, it has to be proved. As I said before, it is most ingenious—most, and it fits all the known circumstances. But even its jolly old author must admit that a great deal of it is purely hypothetical. If the hypothesis should break down—if, for instance, Julep should suddenly turn up with another explanation altogether—you'd have to concoct an entirely fresh reconstruction. But that's no reflection on what you have done. It's a fine bit of work . . .

"And now, Grainger, what about a snooze? We shall have a big day tomorrow. I'm going to see Elburton first, and that will be a delicate and difficult meeting."

"Yes," said Grainger. "Mr Elburton has jumped into the soup tureen this time."

"It wouldn't be a bad idea if you went back to Mrs Colwill's lodgings and resumed the character of the new chauffeur until I've considered what to do. What time do we get to Westport by this train?"

"Half-past four," said Grainger.

"A god-forsaken time! I suppose you could go home and snatch an hour or two in bed, and I could go to the Royal Hotel. Then we could meet, say, at half-past eight and go out to Longbridge in a taxi. It's not much use disturbing the Elburtons before breakfast.

"All right, Mr Pinson, it's your funeral so far, not mine," said Grainger. "But the sooner we get this into the hands of the police and put things regular-like the better I shall be pleased."

II

Mr Grainger reached the Royal Hotel next morning before Mr Pinson was down. But there was a message for him to go up to Mr Pinson's room. Arrived there he heard Mr Pinson splashing water in his bath and singing lustily:

"Je cherche fortune
Autour du Chat Noir,
Au clair de la lune
A Montmartre le soir."

Mr Grainger shook his head. This lawyer friend of his was incorrigibly frivolous. Mr Grainger liked a joke himself, and he loved people to be merry; but this morning he had a horrible weight upon his mind. The prospect of turning that lever, opening that door, inhaling that smell, seeing what there was to be seen, nauseated even Mr Grainger who was accustomed to horrible things.

Yet here was Mr Pinson carolling some French song or other, Mr Grainger could not quite make out what, and apparently as lively as a grig.

Mr Pinson burst into the room in his bath-gown, his hair rumpled and his cheeks rosy, with a "Hello, Grainger! I've had a splendid sleep and feel better than I've felt for days. And hello, Grainger! You look as if you'd just lost a fortune. What's the matter?"

Grainger shook a melancholy head.

"I can't feel merry and bright, Mr Pinson, when I think of what is just in front of us. You know, you've not yet looked inside the door of that strong-room and seen——"

"My dear man," Mr Pinson interrupted him, "neither you nor I nor any friend of ours is inside the strong-room. I didn't know the gentleman, and my only trouble is for the little girl Elburton. But she's young and will get over it. Come—cheer up and let us to breakfast."

"I've had my breakfast," Grainger grumbled.

"Well, then, come and be the death's-head at my feast. Sing dirges and threnodies while I inter the bacon and eggs."

Mr Pinson, who was in irresistibly high spirits, dressed quickly, and they went down to the breakfast-room, where, instead of undertaking the vocal exercises suggested to him, Mr Grainger sipped a cup of coffee and read the morning paper.

At ten o'clock they reached Longbridge. Mr Pinson went first to the Post Office and was closeted with the postmaster for a quarter of an hour. He then went to break the news to the Elburtons. Meanwhile Mr Grainger repaired to Mrs Colwill's lodgings. Mrs Colwill was staggered to see him. She had been slightly staggered when he had not appeared on Monday, as he promised; but now, without a word of warning, to see him arrive at ten o'clock in the morning when she was in the middle of her housework was more staggering than ever. But the most staggering thing of all was that she had not at first been able to recognise Mr Wilson, as he wore mufti, and to see a strange gentleman walk into the place so familiar was—well, Mrs Colwill could not express her feelings though she essayed to do so in a great many words.

However, Mr Wilson had his chauffeur clothes in his bag, and when he could escape from the torrent of her eloquent surprise, he went to his bedroom to change.

Not a word of Mr Julep? No, not a word, she assured him. A strange thing that he should have gone like that and left so many valuables in her possession. But he would turn up to claim them one day, of that she was sure.

Mr Grainger devoutly hoped he would; there was nothing he hoped more.

He was to give Mr Pinson an hour at the bank-house and then to go to Mr Colebroke's, send the servant on a long errand, and volunteer to look after the house till she returned. In the meantime Mrs Paddon would have been lured away by a message from the Elburtons. Thus, they hoped, the place would be clear a sufficient time for their purpose.

Mr Grainger followed this programme. At the appointed time he rang at the door of Mr Colebroke's house and was received by the girl with astonishment.

"Lawks-a-massy!" she cried. We thought you was lost, Mr Wilson."

"Lots of people have tried to lose me, my dear, and never succeeded," he said. "But I've just got a message for you from Mrs Paddon. Will you go to her at the bank-house, Mr Elburton's? And I'm to stand guard over the place while you're gone. She'd be glad if you wouldn't mind calling round to the wool-shop in West Street on the way and getting half a pound of white wool for Miss Elburton."

As the shop in West Street was at the other end of the town, this meant a considerable detour. But it was a fine morning, and the maid was nothing loth.

"Oh, all right, Mr Wilson," she said. "I wonder what Mrs Paddon can want of me up there?"

"I think it's something to do with some affair Miss Elburton is getting up. Is it a bazaar?"

"Haven't heard of any bazaar. But never mind. You'll find the newspaper on the kitchen table."

Mr Grainger got rid of her at last. Then from the shadow of

the Market Hall arches, Mr Pinson and Mr Elburton came quickly across the street. Mr Grainger admitted them, and locked the door.

The three men faced each other in the passage.

"Grainger," said Mr Pinson, "this is Mr Elburton. You know all about his connection with the thing we have in hand. Elburton, I have told you how and why I brought Mr Grainger into the inquiry. You also know of the discovery he has made. Now, we have not too much time. Miss Maud will keep Mrs Paddon and the girl as long as possible, but we must get at the facts completely and decide on our course before she comes back."

"Very well, Mr Pinson," said Grainger. "Let's go up at once."

He led the way up the staircase, followed by Mr Pinson. Elburton, who had not spoken, faltered after them. The locked door of the office presented no difficulty to Grainger. He smashed the lock with a heavy jemmy, which was quicker than picking it, and went into the room.

It was exactly as it had been when Pinson had seen it before —a quiet and dignified room with no symptom of disorder. The green Venetian blinds were drawn against the sun. The glass topped table was dusted and neatly arranged. The telephone stood on its right hand corner. The bookshelves were in perfect order. The panelled end, with the portrait of Mr Colebroke's father, gave no hint of the tragedy it concealed.

"Can you stand it, Elburton?" Mr Pinson asked his friend.

Elburton's face was white, but he nodded for assent.

"Then show us, Grainger," said Mr Pinson.

Grainger walked across to the panelled end of the room, shot back a panel, and disclosed the lever handle which he had described in his reconstruction of the night of the 18th March. The two others stood in the middle of the room, Pinson with his hand on his friend's arm.

Grainger moved the lever and the great iron door swung open, letting out a dull gleam of electric light. The bulb held in the ceiling of the chamber had nearly burnt itself out, and shone with a red glow in its filaments.

Grainger stepped back, and Elburton gave out a little gasping sound as he saw what was on the ground at Grainger's feet.

The body of a man lying on his back, his knees drawn up and his feet on the threshold of the doorway. A dreadful odour slowly drifted out into the room—a strange and penetrating mustiness rather than putridity.

Grainger came away from the door, holding a handkerchief to nose and mouth.

He signed to his companions to leave the room and himself went to the windows and threw them open before he followed them.

"That's poisonous," he said, as they stood on the landing. "Let the air blow through for a few minutes. Mr Pinson, he's nothing but a skeleton. You can see no face, only a black parchment over his skull. He's been there three months, you know."

"Steady, Elburton," said Mr Pinson, as his friend showed signs of giving way. "We'll soon get it over. Smoke!"

He offered cigarettes. Elburton could not smoke. Mr Pinson lit up and Grainger took a pipe from his pocket and blew thick clouds.

"I'll go in and tell you if it's better," he said.

Presently all three advanced to the doorway of the strong-room.

It was as Grainger had said. The poor thing which lay there was hardly the semblance of a man. The features had gone. The nose bone showed sharp through a shining black cuticle. Eyes there were none—only dreadful sockets. The hands, one clutched on the breast, were like the talons of a great bird.

"No identifying him," said Mr Pinson.

"Except by his clothes and anything he may have on him," said Grainger. "But we had better not touch. That's a job for the police and the doctors. Have you seen enough?"

Elburton clutched Mr Pinson's arm and stumbled out of the room, half fainting. Grainger closed the strong-room door and followed.

"I am going home with Mr Elburton," said Mr Pinson. "If you

will wait here, Grainger, I will come back to you, and we can arrange about reporting to the police. I will see that Mrs Paddon and the maid stay where they are."

III

Returning alone to the house within twenty minutes, Mr Pinson said,

"Now, Grainger, before we get Mr Bluecoat on the scene, I want to have a good look at it myself. Under the circumstances, I had to bring Elburton down. But of course he is not used to this frightfulness, and one could not go into the realities while he was here."

"What do you mean by going into the realities?" asked Grainger.

"Well, I want to examine your theory of the crime on the spot, to test it by every test there is and to come to a conclusion about it. Don't forget, my dear Grainger, that I am acting for Elburton all through, and that, owing to what you rightly called his folly, he stands in a very ticklish position. I want to be forearmed as fully as possible. When the police butt in, what are the odds that they want to arrest Elburton? I know you have your mind full of the chauffeur fellow; but it doesn't follow that everybody's mind will be equally full of him."

Mr Grainger gaped his astonishment.

"I can't make you out, Mr Pinson," he said. "I'll bet you any money that nobody ever dreams of arresting Mr Elburton, or even of suspecting him."

"Nevertheless, Grainger, we'll do as I say. We want a better light up there, and I've brought an electric torch. So now."

They went to the chamber where that horror lay. Mr Pinson stepped over it into the strong-room and illuminated it with his torch.

A real strong-room this. The walls of huge stone blocks, finely cut and pointed with cement. The iron door four inches thick, mounted in a great iron frame upon enormous hinges. Mr

Pinson took his pen-knife and tried to make an indentation in the cement. Its point broke off.

Around the walls a shelf with cupboards beneath. Mr Pinson opened one or two. They contained little—a few papers and books of account. In a corner a small pile of deed-boxes.

On the shelf, however, an object which Mr Pinson examined closely. A cash-box of the common kind, open, empty, with a smashed lock. He did not touch it. Throwing the beam of his torch upon it, he said to Grainger, looking through the doorway,

"That should have finger-prints and be a valuable exhibit."

Grainger nodded.

"Now, Grainger, show me your theory. I'll be Colebroke coming into the room and going to the place where my three thousand pounds should be waiting for me. You be Julep, concealed in the strong-room. I switch off the light. Get inside, and see how you can conceal yourself by crouching or any other method. I will advance as you say Colebroke did."

Grainger entered the chamber, and Mr Pinson came out. Grainger pulled the door close and left his companion alone in the office. Mr Pinson walked from the door to the strong-room, entered, pressed down the switch, and went towards the shelf where the cash-box stood. When he turned, Grainger was out in the office, facing him and pointing a revolver. He pressed the trigger twice, the second time as Mr Pinson reached the doorway by stepping gingerly over the body.

"Yes, Grainger, it could be done. You got out cleverly. We'll assume Julep was equally clever. But let me draw your attention to one thing: Colebroke must have known as soon as he entered the office that somebody was in the strong-room.

"How?"

"The door was not completely closed when you went in."

But it might have been, Grainger pointed out, for on the inside there was a second lever corresponding with the one behind the panel, which would give anybody inside the power of egress.

"M-m," said Mr Pinson. "That is so. If a man got shut in accidentally he could let himself out. Yes, I see. Where was it you found the flattened bullet, Grainger?"

Mr Pinson was shown the little hole in the woodwork close to the hinge of the door. The bullet had, in fact, flattened itself against the iron framework.

"Rather high, as well as out of lateral aim, don't you think?" said Mr Pinson.

"I expect his nerves were rather jumpy," Grainger replied. "Surprising if they weren't, wouldn't it be?"

Mr Pinson admitted it. He walked to and fro in the office for a minute or two, gazing at the carpet, and deep in thought.

"Well, Grainger," he said at last. "I suppose we may as well shut it up and give the information to the police. There seems to be nothing more to learn in this room. You can do all that is necessary. I want to be with the Elburtons when inquiries are made of them. You may as well ring up the police, tell them who you are, and get them here. Do you happen to know the superintendent?"

"Catlin? Oh yes, I know him very well. No difficulty there."

"All right then, Grainger. Mind, I'm acting for Elburton alone. I have no other interest in the affair, and I don't care twopence who the murderer is so long as suspicion does not fall on him. So don't expect any help from me if you get involved in the chase for Julep."

Mr Grainger's nerves were jangling that day. His temper seemed short.

"Look here, Mr Pinson," said he, "I know you don't do anything without a reason, and it's generally a pretty good one. But you're keeping me in the dark about something. Is it quite fair?"

"My dear Grainger," Mr Pinson replied, "as between friends, I'm not keeping you in the dark about anything it is possible for me to tell you. I'm greatly obliged for your help, and you've been invaluable to me. Now that things have reached this stage, I know you can't simply clear out and leave the case alone. I wish you could. But a nod's as good as a wink, eh? Of course, so far as you are bound to go you may rely on me for expenses. But don't go any further than you're obliged."

Having thus cryptically delivered himself, Mr Pinson went off to the bank-house, and Mr Grainger turned to the telephone.

Mr Pinson discovered Elburton collapsed in his office chair, and left him there with the assurance that the sensation would be short and sharp, and that public attention would soon be directed from him in another direction.

He then went to seek Miss Maud, who was talking white wool and jumpers to Mrs Paddon, while the maid waited with Elburton's servants in the kitchen. At a sign from him, Miss Maud left him alone with the housekeeper.

It was a difficult thing Mr Pinson had to do. He must break to her the news of that horror with which she had unknowingly been living for three months. He did it somehow, and when she departed with the girl her agitation was over.

She found the police in possession of Mr Colebroke's house, and Superintendent Catlin in close conclave in the office with Wilson the chauffeur.

IV

Mr Pinson proved perfect in his prediction to Elburton. As soon as the news spread through Longbridge that Mr Westmore Colebroke had been found murdered in his own house, where the body had lain undiscovered for three months the first thought of everybody who knew of their relations and of Elburton's pretence that Colebroke had gone away on private business held a momentary suspicion of him. It was with the utmost pains that the excellent superintendent of police was prevented from "detaining" the bank manager for inquiries. It was part of the subject of his long conclave with Mr Grainger in the office. But both Grainger and Mr Pinson having given assurances that Elburton would detain himself and be at the disposal of the police whenever he was wanted, they contrived to shunt Mr Catlin on to the track of the chauffeur Julep.

The first sitting of the Coroner's inquest was held the same evening in one of the dingy apartments of the Market Hall across the street. Mr Pinson appeared to say that he had been instructed to watch the proceedings on behalf of Mr Elburton, whose name would undoubtedly be mentioned in the course of the inquiry.

The Coroner nodded assent, and said that the course he proposed was to call only evidence of identification now, and to take a long adjournment. He understood that the police needed much time for inquiry. The body could be buried after the medical evidence had been given. The jury had already seen it. He would first call Elizabeth Paddon.

Mrs Paddon, who had been sitting at the back of the room, was ushered to a seat by the Coroner's side at the table. She was flushed and worried.

"Mrs Paddon," said the Coroner, "we know this is a very painful thing for you, and we wish to spare you as much as possible."

"Thank you, Dr Grey," she murmured. "I know you are always very considerate."

The Coroner looked a little shocked, as if it were quite out of order that Mrs Paddon should have discovered that the official of the law before whom she appeared was really her favourite doctor whose mixture did her winter bronchitis so much good.

"We shall probably have to put to you more detailed questions at a later date," he said. "But for the present, if you will give me the few facts for which I ask, it will be enough. Now, you have seen the body which lay in the strong-room at No. 45 High Street today?"

"Yes, sir."

"Do you identify it as the body of Westmore Colebroke?"

"So far as I could see, sir, it was. I could not recognise him—nobody could, if I may say so, sir, by anything but his clothes."

"But you recognised the clothes?"

"Yes, sir—a blue serge suit, of the kind he always wore."

"When did you last see him alive?"

"On the evening of the 18th of March, sir."

"And where?"

"At his own dinner-table, sir. He dined at home as usual that night. And when I went in to ask whether there was anything more he wanted, he said 'No'; he had dined very well, and he was going along to Mr Elburton's for a little music, as he often did. He said he might be late, and I wasn't to wait up for him."

"Was that usual or unusual?"

"Oh, quite usual, sir. He often stayed till after eleven at Mr Elburton's—he was that fond of the music," Mrs Paddon answered, her voice quivering a little.

"Did he seem quite normal—I mean cheerful? He was an equable-tempered man as a rule. Nothing seemed to be worrying or disturbing him?"

"Nothing at all, sir. He was as merry as ever—and a merrier, nicer gentleman never was." Mrs Paddon was on the point of giving way to her feelings.

"So," said the Coroner, "you and the maid went to bed. You heard nothing in the night?"

"Nothing whatever, sir."

"No sound of any dispute, or any shots?"

"Not a sound, sir."

"And in the morning, what happened?"

"Rose—that's the maid—went to call him at the usual time, half-past seven. She got no answer, and came and told me. I said to wait till eight and then go again. She did, and there was no answer."

"What did you do?"

"I went myself and knocked, and as I heard nothing I went in. Mr Colebroke was not there, and his bed had not been slept in."

"And then, I believe, you went to inform Mr Elburton?"

"Yes, sir, and he——"

"You needn't tell us now anything that passed between you. That will come later. Have you anything you would like to ask this witness, Mr Pinson?"

Mr Pinson shook his head and smiled encouragingly to Mrs Paddon, who was immediately released from the table, to be succeeded by Superintendent Catlin.

The police officer's evidence was cast in the customary form. From information received he had gone to No. 45 High Street, and there had seen the body in such and such circumstances, and had called Dr Mayfield to examine it.

"Henry Mayfield," the Coroner called, looking at the list before him as if he had never heard the name before, though the young doctor who stepped to the witness chair was his very good crony and the only other practitioner in the place, who shared with him the business of healing the sick and coddling the fanciful on well-understood terms.

Dr Mayfield gave his full name and address and his degrees and qualifications, all of which were solemnly and laboriously written down by the Coroner. He had, he said, been called by the police to No. 45 High Street at 11.46 that morning. Pinson smiled at the minute particularity. He had there seen the body of a man lying in the open doorway of a sort of strong-room which seemed ordinarily to be hidden behind the panel of the wall. The man had been dead a long time, probably several months. He could not say exactly how long. The flesh had decayed, and though covered with a cuticle the body was practically a skeleton. The portion of the body was peculiar. It lay on its back thus—and he showed its relation to the door by means of the testament on the table—with the knees drawn up and the feet on the very threshold.

"Did you recognise the body?" asked the Coroner.

"No. It was quite unrecognisable. Not a feature could be identified."

"You knew Westmore Colebroke well?"

"Yes, very well."

"Is it in your opinion probable that the body you have described is that of Mr Colebroke?"

"I have no doubt that it is."

"Perhaps you will tell us how you arrive at that conclusion?"

"Well," said Dr Mayfield, "all the general indications are there. The body was clothed in such garments as Mr Colebroke usually wore—a blue suit and a double collar with a flowing bow tie. I looked at the tailors' mark on the coat-hanger. It was that of the Westport tailors Cozens, and I know Colebroke got his clothes there. Though there was no possibility of recognising the face, the body had possessed a short dark brown beard such as Colebroke wore. I judge also by the height of the body and the figure."

"That," said the Coroner, "is as far as you can go, but subject to the reservations you have made you identify the body as that of Westmore Colebroke?"

"I do."

"Can you tell us the cause of death?"

"No. I have not had time to make more than a superficial examination. With a corpse in such a condition, it is difficult. I shall need assistance and time."

"You could not say at present whether the deceased came to his end by violence or otherwise; I mean, you have not been able to determine whether the body bears any marks of wounding?"

"No," said the doctor, "I can say nothing on that point till I have made a very thorough post-mortem."

And with this the eager public and the newspaper men had to be content. The Coroner announced that he would adjourn the inquest for a fortnight, and that in the meantime, when the medical evidence had been completed, he would give an order for burial of the body. The facts disclosed were handed over to the Press for speculation and comment, and to the police for inquiry, with the assistance of Mr Grainger, and the Longbridge mystery became the current Nine Days Wonder.

How did Colebroke die? Who killed him? Or was he killed? What were the police doing to allow the grass to grow under their feet for three months? Why had not a crime been suspected when the circumstances were so suspicious?

Where was the chauffeur Julep? The garrulity of various people on the subject of Julep and his characteristics provided the journalists with their best material.

When it leaked out somehow or other that a bullet-mark had been found in the room the hue and cry for Julep became intense.

V

These proceedings seemed not to possess a particle of interest for Mr Pinson. He concerned himself alone with their effect upon the Elburton family. Mr Elburton was in a state of nervous collapse, wrought to a pitch of agonised grief by the death of his friend, worried by the publicity of his own connection with the story, and above all afflicted by the extraordinary revelation which he now received of the callousness and indifference of his daughter's character.

"It breaks my heart, Pinson," he said. "This girl, soft, affectionate, everything I would have had a girl of mine until now—and I thought she was fond of Colebroke: I was sure of it! At any rate, she could not have failed to see that he was passionately fond of her. Yet she seems to take no notice whatever of this horrible thing. She is hardly sorry!"

"My dear Elburton," said Pinson, "I beg you not to give way. If it in as you say, you ought to be glad your girl is saved so much pain. You may have been wrong as to her feeling for Colebroke. You may be wrong now. Women have ways of concealing what they feel. Anyhow, you shouldn't worry. I have a suggestion to make to you. Let Miss Maud come and stay with my wife in London for a bit. You won't want to leave till after the inquest, of course, but she would be better out of this atmosphere. I can promise you both a happy issue out of your afflictions. Only have patience."

"If she would go——" Elburton began.

"Oh, she would go if you pressed her and assured her that you would be more comfortable with her away."

"I'll try her," he answered.

Mr Pinson had no doubt about the result of Elburton's approach to Miss Maud. He had talked to her already. The morning after the inquest he had found her in the garden.

"The secret is still a secret, I suppose?" he had asked.

"Yes, a solemn secret," she replied.

Mr Pinson looked hard at her as she walked by his side.

"Your father is worried," said he, "because he does not understand. I do not think he ought to be worried, Miss Maud. If you cannot tell him the secret, better take it away for a time."

She looked up anxiously.

"What do you mean?"

"I mean, go away yourself for a while, so that he may not be constantly speculating and puzzling, as he does every time he sees you. Come to London and stay with Mrs Pinson for a week or two. I assure you it is the best way. You are very young and very loyal, and you can't be expected to grasp all that this business means to older people. You know me a little, and you will believe me when I say I mean to see that every bit of anxiety I can save your father is spared. I assure you, too, that you can help if you will do what I suggest."

So it was that when Mr Elburton spoke of the subject to his daughter he found her quite ready to go. The idea of leaving him brought into her dark eyes tears, which had not been there when she heard the news of Colebroke's death. But Pinson's argument had prevailed.

They left together that afternoon, and within a few hours Miss Elburton was installed in the Adelphi flat and had made the acquaintance of Mrs Pinson. The Honourable Dora having already retired, the introduction to her was postponed until the morning.

"A nice thing for ladies to do after dinner," said Mr Pinson, when Irene had finally clattered out of the room, "is to sit by an open window and listen to a story—if the teller has the virtues of wit, humour and literary excellence, which I flatter myself I possess."

"The Lord of Creation commands his dutiful subjects to sit and be bored while he practises his next speech to the jury," said Mrs Pinson. "Miss Elburton, shall we rebel and retire to the sitting-room for some music, and let him address the chimney-pots in John Street?"

"Rebellion is useless," said Mr Pinson. "All the approaches

are guarded, and the victims are helpless. Besides, music will probably wake up the Honourable Dora Pinson. Miss Maud, take no notice of any insults levelled at me by my wife. She is dying to hear my voice. Here is the most comfortable chair. My wife likes uncomfortable chairs because they remind her of her glorious days of freedom as a typist before she became enslaved to me. Also, I beg you to note that Mrs Pinson has a gruesome taste in stories. There is not enough violent death in the Arabian Nights to satisfy her, and she rather fancies herself a female Vidocq at unravelling mysteries."

"Never mind him, Miss Elburton," said Mrs Pinson. "It's only his way. I suppose he has some glimmering of an idea in his brain if one could only see it for the cloud of words."

"My idea," said Mr Pinson, standing with his cigarette in hand and looking down on the two ladies, "is to entertain you with a confidential story. I would not tell it to anybody but you two. My wife will worry it out of me anyhow, and Miss Maud knows part of it. I am going to tell you a story which in a fortnight's time or less will be common property. It will be in all the newspapers. It is the real solution of the Longbridge mystery——"

Miss Maud started from her chair.

"Mr Pinson!" she cried.

He took her hand and persuaded her to be seated again.

"Miss Maud—anything said in this room is as if it had never been said. Besides, I remind you that the whole thing will be public in a very few days. And it is necessary that you and I should perfectly understand each other.

"The simple explanation of the Longbridge Mystery is that there is no mystery at all. I will tell you what happened, and if at any point within your knowledge I am wrong, you shall correct me."

The girl sat with head in hands as she had done in the garden at Longbridge.

"Not long after Mr Westmore Colebroke returned from Paris to take up his father's practice in Longbridge, he fell in love with Miss Maud Elburton and she fell in love with him," Mr Pinson began.

"My dear!" exclaimed Mrs Pinson, impulsively kneeling in front of the girl and clasping her.

"No need for heroics," said Mr Pinson. "I beg half the audience to resume its seat. Well, the course of true love ran perfectly smooth, with a musical accompaniment. It sounds something like a romantic opera, doesn't it?"

"Noel!" Mrs Pinson cried, looking at him in indignant puzzlement.

"Well, let us be getting on without interruptions ," he said. "Mr Westmore Colebroke disappeared on the night of the 18th March. Miss Elburton had great difficulty in preserving a straight face when she saw how that evanishment was worrying her father. Because she was perfectly well aware that Mr Colebroke was going to disappear, and why. He had told her all about it.

"Now, she might be able to conceal the fact of her knowledge from her father; but she could not hide it from the lynx-eye of Mr Noel Pinson, who discovered it not many hours after he had the honour of making her delightful acquaintance. Not only did Miss Maud know that Mr Colebroke intended to disappear, and why—but also where. And she knew that he certainly had no intention of disappearing into his own strong-room. Far from it —very far—hundreds of miles!"

"But, Noel——" Mrs Pinson began.

"Silence in court!" Mr Pinson retorted. "If there are any more interruptions, I will clear the court. To resume: When Mr Westmore Colebroke's body was discovered in the strong-room, nobody was less surprised than Miss Maud."

"More surprised, you mean——"

"No. I mean exactly what I say. For Miss Maud was aware, by incontestable evidence, that it was not the body of Mr Colebroke, but somebody else's, and as the only body in which she was greatly interested, apart from her father, was Mr Colebroke, the discovery left her unmoved."

"Not Mr Colebroke!" Mrs Pinson broke in. "Then whose—

whom—who, I mean?"

"At present, the body has been identified as that of Mr Colebroke, and when it becomes known that the witnesses have proved the impossible, it will be necessary to begin the process of identification all over again. I have a shrewd suspicion, but I am not going to commit myself. I was called in to help Elburton, and having proved that he could have had nothing to do with the death of Colebroke, who isn't dead, I don't want to worry about who is dead. That is, at the present time. The rest depends on the police—as to how intelligent or unintelligent their action may be.

"So I come to my motive for telling you this story in this particular way. What the police will do depends very much upon Miss Maud."

The girl looked up at him.

"Upon me?" she asked.

"Yes. If you do not allow certain facts to become known, they will get a verdict from the coroner's jury that Mr Westmore Colebroke was murdered. They may even be able to throw suspicion of the murder upon somebody. They will certainly chase all over the world after somebody. And are you going to let them?"

"You know I can do nothing, Mr Pinson. I will certainly never speak—unless a man is in danger of his life."

"I thought you would say that. But if a man is?"

"How can he be," asked the girl, "seeing that he is already dead?"

Mr Pinson started back.

"Ah—so you have identified the corpse yourself?" he said.

"I have no doubt that the dead man is Julep the chauffeur."

Mr Pinson took two or three turns across the little room.

"The dead man was wearing Mr Colebroke's clothes."

"Yes. Mr Colebroke regularly gave away to his servants the suits which he had half worn out and many other things. Julep was a taciturn man, but, up to a certain time, Mr Colebroke liked him, and he was an excellent driver. Mr Colebroke was very kind to him."

"But," said Mrs Pinson, "the papers state that Julep was a clean-shaven man, and at the inquest it was said there were signs of a brown beard."

"That," said Mr Pinson, "is nothing. A man's beard will grow when he is dead. But here we have the heart of your problem, Miss Maud. Let me elaborate the story a little. Our hero, Colebroke, told his sweetheart in March of a danger he was running, and pledged her to secrecy about it. He told her also that Julep, for a disgraceful action, had been dismissed. Their relations were no longer friendly. What is Miss Maud going to do when this comes out, and Mr Colebroke is accused, as he certainly will be, of murdering Julep?"

"Ah!" cried the girl. "How fantastic! How impossible! Why, nobody knows anything about it."

"Then how do I know?" said Pinson. "It is known; it cannot be hidden; a letter in which Mr Colebroke speaks of it is probably already in the possession of the police—found among the belongings of Julep. There is your problem, Miss Maud. It isn't easy. I merely want to forewarn you that you may have to face it."

"But you don't believe, Mr Pinson, that Westmore murdered Julep? Why should he do it? It's absurd."

"Absolutely. I am quite certain he didn't. But to prove it, that secret will have to be a secret no longer. I tell you what—I'll bet you that the secret comes out, very soon too, and that when it does it will be found that there has been no reason in the world for keeping it secret!"

"You bewilder me," said the girl. "You seem to know even more than I do. But I dare not say a word. I *won't* say a word!" she exclaimed. "I will never speak of it until I am released from my promise."

"Of course you won't. I didn't expect you to. I just show you where you stand and what you have to face. Now I hope you'll stay here and forget as much as you can in the company of Mrs Pinson. I also am going to disappear for a day or two. But be home to meet me without fail on Thursday evening for dinner at eight and another little chat after dinner, won't you?"

VI

The police came under the customary severe and unreasonable criticism because they had no immediate solution of the Longbridge mystery and nobody had been arrested. The criticism increased in severity as it declined in reasonableness. But the police plodded along the appointed line of inquiry and took good care to arrest nobody until they had some shadow of suspicion to throw upon the criminal.

"False arrests," said Mr Catlin to a "crime investigator" from a newspaper office, "are worse than no arrests, and if you take my advice you will keep out of this. Any butting in which interferes with our work will mean an unpleasant quarter of an hour for somebody."

Mr Catlin admitted that he had a clue, but refused to give even the merest hint of its nature. He was particularly careful not to reveal Mr Grainger to the "investigators," for it was on Mr Grainger that the pursuit of the clue depended.

On the morning after the inquest opened, Mr Grainger had received an urgent telephonic summons from his friend at Scotland Yard. He reached London in the fewest possible hours. The Chief of the CID had become deeply interested in the Longbridge affair, he was informed, and it was upon special instructions from that lofty quarter that he had been sent for.

The Chief received him in his office alone.

"I have been told about you, Mr Grainger," he said. "I heard of you in connection with a former case. Now, you have all the strings of this one in your hands, I believe?"

Mr Grainger thought he knew all there was to be known about it.

"I see the police are coming in for the usual abuse, Mr Grainger. Well, the more we are abused the better, so long as we pull through. Now, will you become a policeman again for this occasion, and work with Scotland Yard?"

"I'm afraid I can hardly do that, sir—officially. I'm privately employed, and with certain instructions."

The Chief eyed him closely.

"Well, I'm not going to ask you what those instructions are or from whom you get them. But you will admit, of course, that the public interest demands the solution of this business and that justice must come first. You cannot refuse to give us your help."

"Certainly not, sir," said Mr Grainger. "I have my own ideas, and I understand they are confirmed by what the Yard has discovered. Unofficially I put myself entirely at your service."

"Very well, Mr Grainger. Then, we have a very strong clue to the wanted man Julep, and we wish to follow it up. You have already seen the woman, and you can see her again in the same character. She will be less suspicious with you than if we approach her from a fresh angle. And it is up to you to get from her the essential information. They have all the material in the office, and two of our best men will be at your disposal. Let's have Julep in the shortest possible time."

Mr Grainger wondered, after this conversation, whether Mr Pinson would approve of the course he was taking. But he felt a personal pique towards the discovery and the arrest of Julep. For the time he dismissed Mr Pinson from his thoughts.

The material in the office was certainly very suggestive. It established the fact that within a day or two, at Camberwell, the woman Bella had been in secret communication with a man whose acquaintance she carefully concealed from her present protector. The man, who was unknown to the neighbourhood, appeared to have watched for an opportunity when the greengrocer was away from his business and to have had a long interview with her in the room behind the shop. This interview ended in a quarrel. The loud dispute drew the attention of neighbours, and was partly overheard by a girl employed by the greengrocer. It was a dispute about money and letters. The only available description of the man came from this girl, and was rather vague; but it would correspond with the account of Julep's appearance that had been published. The significant thing was that the man was a taxi-driver, and had arrived with his vehicle and driven away in it. Unfortunately, nobody had taken the number of the taxi.

Mr Grainger absorbed this information and realised its importance. If the taxi-driver was Julep, probably he had been in London at this employment since he left Longbridge; but now that there was a hue and cry in the papers he would go to ground. The quickest way to trace him was through the woman Bella, if she could be induced to speak. And Mr Grainger thought he could induce her to speak.

A visit to the shop in Camberwell that night was blank. Mrs Findlater—it appeared that the greengrocer was Findlater, though he was known as Camberwell Greengrocers, Ltd.—had gone out for the evening and there was no knowing what time she would be home. Mr Grainger, impatient of the delay, devoted himself to some fruitless inquiries in the neighbourhood, which knew not Julep, and then had to be content with inaction till next day.

Watching the opportunity of Mr Findlater's absence, on business or pleasure, on the following morning, Mr Grainger entered the shop and within two minutes had Miss Bella Waters at his mercy.

"You lied to me the other day," he said. "Don't lie now. No—" as the woman bridled in protest, "there's no time for any nonsense. You've got to be straight. You've seen the papers. You know that Julep's neck is in danger. I must see him. Where is he?"

"I don't know anything about him," she said sullenly.

"And you haven't seen him for three months?"

"No."

"You are a poor liar," said Mr Grainger. He pointed his finger at her and said sternly,

"You saw him last night! Where is he?"

The woman burst into weeping.

"If you do not tell me, I shall wait till Mr Findlater comes back, and insist on an explanation from him."

She sprang up and cried,

"Oh! Now we know where we are, Mr Sneak. You pretend to be a friend of Julep's. But you're a dirty police dog, that's what you are!—nosing around and trying to smell out mischief. Tell Mr Findlater, will you? All right. So you can. I kept nothing back from Mr Findlater. He knows all about Julep, and all about you—see? You don't get me that way. I call it dirty, that's what I do."

Mr Grainger recoiled from this attack, but soon recovered himself. Having been invested by Miss Waters, or Mrs Findlater —whichever she was—with the character of a policeman, he immediately assumed it. He knew now that he was perfectly certain to get the information he wanted. The shot he had aimed into the blue had gone home.

"Very well, Mrs Findlater," said he. "Well, suppose I am a policeman. Whether I am or not, I mean to find out where Julep is. You know he is wanted in connection with a crime. Either he is guilty or he is not. If he is not guilty, let him come out and explain. If he is and you conceal him, do you know what your position is? Accessory after the fact—that's what they call it in law. It means that you are equally guilty with him if you do not tell what you know. Another thing—Mr Findlater is accessory after the fact, and we shall want him too. Another thing—do you know where that money came from? If you don't, I do. Now, what about it?"

During this harangue, in which Mr Grainger had transgressed every rule of legal police procedure, he had watched the woman's face very carefully. What made her blench was the assertion that Mr Findlater might be dragged in as an accessory.

"What about it?" Mr Grainger repeated.

VII

Mr Grainger, if he had been giving evidence, would have said that it was "from information received." A more exact statement would have been that it was from information extracted by menaces. But, however it was, as the result of the information, he and his two officers from Scotland Yard alighted that afternoon on the bridge at Westbourne Park Station and told the taxi-man to wait there until he was called again.

They then strolled separately into the vague region of mean streets which lies between Westbourne Park and Portobello Road and is one of the strangest phenomena of West London. In the dirtiest and dreariest of the slums—a street of dingy grey houses, with cracked plaster walls and a noisy population of half-clad urchins—they met before a door, and, without exchanging a word, entered and walked up the stone staircase, Mr Grainger leading the procession. Mr Grainger had a revolver in his hip-pocket, and as he reached a door on the second floor he took it out. The two officers were also holding similar weapons in their hands when they stopped in front of that door.

No doubt the dingy house had witnessed scenes of violence in the course of its deplorable career, but probably never such a display of armed force. Whoever was on the other side of the door was to be effectively overawed.

Mr Grainger tried the handle silently.

"Not locked," he whispered. "Now then!"

He threw the door open and cried,

"Hands up, Julep!"

The man who had been seated at a table looking over some papers while he smoked a cigarette, turned and saw the muzzles of three pistols directed at his head. He went on puffing his cigarette and paid no attention to Mr Grainger's invitation. It was Mr Grainger who exclaimed,

"Well I'm d——d!"

He lowered his revolver and put it away, and at a sign from him his companions followed suit.

"Delighted to see you, Grainger," said Mr Pinson. "Won't you all come in? Sorry there are not enough chairs for everybody. Our friend Julep apparently expected visitors, because he is not here. No doubt he had insufficient time to make any hospitable preparations before he left."

"But, Mr Pinson!" cried Grainger, "what does it mean?"

"I should say, Grainger, it means that the ex-chauffeur had a wonderful olfactory sense. He smelt a rat."

"Yes, of course. But—you here?"

"Oh—I? You know what an irresponsible person I am. I expect the reason for my presence is precisely the same as yours. I wanted to have a little chat with Mr Julep—to exchange impressions with him about what the newspapers call the Longbridge mystery. But when I called he was out, and I imagine the date and time of his return are exceedingly uncertain."

"The bird's flown!" said Mr Grainger.

"That's a rhetorical way of putting it. Yes—the bird has flown," said Mr Pinson. "I've been taking a look round its nest. If these gentlemen, whom I seem to recognise, are from Scotland Yard, they will like to have a look round too. But I'm afraid they will find very little corn left. These seem to be the only papers—three letters from proprietors of motor-cars briefly regretting that they cannot accept Mr Julep's services as chauffeur."

"He used his own name, then!" said Mr Grainger.

"Strangely enough, he did. Very likely if he had called himself Atkins or Smith, he would have been engaged. Julep is such a difficult name to call out without feeling bilious, isn't it?"

The officers from Scotland Yard regarded Mr Pinson with astonishment. They looked, in fact, as if they had their suspicions about him, but as Mr Grainger had been put in charge of them by High Places, they said nothing.

Mr Grainger looked to his employer for a lead, and Mr Pinson, perceiving the fact, gave it.

"I should like to have a yarn with you, Grainger, while your friends are examining Julep's lair. Could you give me half an hour or so?

Mr Grainger thought he could. He instructed the officers to discover all they could in the room and in the neighbourhood and fixed a time to meet them again. Then he and Mr Pinson left together.

"Shall we walk while we talk?" said Mr Pinson. "So you've been dragged right into it, Grainger? No keeping out?"

"No, it was impossible," he replied. "CID got hold of me, and I could not refuse. But I'm still in the dark about you, Mr Pinson. What does it mean?"

"Why, there's no mystery about it. You remember that you formed one theory and I formed another. You are pursuing your theory, and I am chasing mine, and they've led us both to North Kensington—that's all. If you were not in with the CID I might be able to throw a little more light upon your doubts, Grainger; but as you are in the official hunt, I cannot."

"I see that. But I still don't understand what brought you up here. You must have been on Julep's trail before we were. I don't begin to see how you picked it up."

"One day," said Mr Pinson, "I'll tell you. At present my chief anxiety is to know what you are going to do next. Because on that depends what I shall do next."

Mr Grainger walked along for a few moments in silence.

"I think the next thing I shall do is to get Miss Bella Waters under lock and key as an accessory after the fact," he said.

Mr Pinson was thoughtful too, and did not reply at once.

"It's rather like a policeman's notion, Mr Grainger," said he. "I wonder . . . How are you going to get proof of her accessory knowledge?"

"That's an easy one," said Grainger. "The money."

"What money?"

"The money that Julep sent to her."

"Ah, he'd sent her money, had he?" said Mr Pinson.

"Ah, but of course he had. Remember the letter? When I learned that a man who resembled Julep had been visiting Miss Bella Waters, I guessed it was the money he wanted. It was. And he didn't get it. Miss Bella Waters has tied herself up in knots over this business."

"You astonish me, my dear Grainger," said Mr Pinson. "Unravel them for me, will you?"

"Oh, it was quite easy. I guessed the money. Because he came to see her and there was a row, I guessed she had not shelled out. And putting two and two together, I guessed the reason—which was, that Mr Findlater had it and refused to part."

"Worthy, provident greengrocer!" murmured Mr Pinson.

"So I tackled Mr Findlater himself and put the fear of the Lord into him, and it all came out. The money was a hundred pounds. It was sent to Miss Bella Waters at a moment when she was beginning to be infatuated with Mr Findlater. She could not keep her secret, but Mr Findlater kept the hundred pounds all right. He even passed it into his bank, because Miss Bella Waters might have difficulty in dealing with such a sum in such a form."

"And so you went to the bank?" said Mr Pinson. "It was the Camberwell branch of the London and Great Eastern, and you found that the £100 note No. AA606751 had been lodged by Mr Findlater on such and such a date, and you knew through Catlin's inquiries at Longbridge that this was one of the notes Colebroke had drawn on the day before he disappeared. It was very clever of you, Grainger."

Mr Grainger stopped in the middle of the pavement and looked at his companion.

"But you—Mr Pinson! You know it all already! Why, I came here straight from the bank!"

"Quite so, Grainger: quite so, I don't doubt it. But you see, I had been to the bank before, so that's why it wasn't new to me."

"And, knowing all this, you still doubt Julep's guilt?"

"Haven't got half enough information yet," said Mr Pinson, "to talk about anybody's guilt, Least of all, Miss Bella Waters's. Still, my dear fellow, if you must arrest somebody, arrest her by all means. If it has no other effect, it will give Findlater a fright. And as he's a nasty avaricious person, I shan't weep about that. But you must give up calling her Miss Bella Waters. She's married Findlater."

"Again, I can't make you out, Mr Pinson—"

"Sorry, Grainger. But you're on the side of officialdom now, you know. I've explained my simple position to you. I don't mind. Go straight ahead. We shall meet at Philippi—I mean at the inquest when it is resumed. Don't worry about me. You carry on with the official case: now that you are in it, that will be the best course from my point of view. Ah—here's Westbourne Park. I'll leave you to return to your friends back there. By the way, send me your copies of those letters you took from the Leducs at Longbridge, will you? Can I have them at the Adelphi tonight?"

"Yes, of course. But I've half a mind to throw it up and chance what the Chief says." Mr Grainger looked partly annoyed and wholly puzzled.

"No. Don't be an ass, Grainger. Look after your own interests. Au revoir."

"I can hardly think it's my interest to be working at cross purposes with you . . ." he began.

But Mr Pinson was turning into the station lobby.

"Au revoir," said he. "Don't forget the letters."

That evening the newspapers published a blurred paragraph under Stop Press News to the effect that in connection with the Longbridge mystery the London police had detained a woman on suspicion of being an accessory, and that she would possibly be brought before the magistrates at Longbridge the next day.

And in the morning the story of the detention of Mrs Findlater was embellished with very large headlines and a great wealth of black type, and there were photographs of the establishment of Camberwell Greengrocers, Ltd., of the front of the bank where the £100 note had been lodged, and a variety of equally relevant matters.

"Now," said the public, "they'll soon be on the track of Julep," and commended the police as handsomely as it had formerly condemned them fiercely.

VIII

Mr Pinson, on leaving Mr Grainger, had strolled leisurely into the lobby of Westbourne Park Station. He strolled leisurely through it and out at another door. Perceiving that Mr Grainger had already turned the corner, he threw off his lethargy, and called to a lingering taxi-driver, who drew up to the pavement.

"Camberwell . . . Drive like hell," said Mr Pinson. The man stared at him. "No—not a mad poet," said he, "quite an accident.

Get on with it quickly."

He pulled the door behind him. The taxi buzzed away. Through the window Mr Pinson saw a kaleidoscope of London—the Park, the Mall, Westminster, Vauxhall, and finally the maze of South London streets—and his cab pulled up in front of Camberwell Greengrocers, Ltd.

"Wait," said he to the driver, and walked through the shop as if he owned it to the room behind.

Mrs Findlater sat there, looking moody. She sprang up as he entered.

"Ah, Mrs Findlater," said Mr Pinson. "Excuse my abrupt entry, but I'm in a hurry. You've had a visitor today, I believe."

"A dirty sneak!" cried Mrs Findlater.

"Ah well, I wouldn't go as far as that. A gentleman with a fixed idea in his head, shall we say? Now, I want it kept there. You're going to have another visit from him—very soon. I can't say how soon: may be in a quarter of an hour. You're going to be arrested, Mrs Findlater. You can try to escape, but it will only prolong the agony. If I may offer you a little advice, it is that you should say nothing and go quietly. When I say nothing, I mean nothing argumentative. Of course you can tell him you're not guilty, and if it gives you any satisfaction, by all means call him a dirty sneak. But I came to warn you and to cheer you up. There will be some inconvenience and some notoriety: I don t see how you can avoid it. The truth will come out in a few days, and then you'll be able to crow over them all, eh? My point is—don't give them the slightest assistance by any unguarded remark. Abuse them to your heart's content, but not a word about the case."

"It's all very well for you——" Mrs Findlater began.

"My dear lady," said Mr Pinson, "I can't stay to argue. When one is up against it, you know, one has to stand up to it. That's all I ask you. I can't stop them in their misplaced desire to see you under lock and key. I would if I could. I only want to assure you that there is no real danger."

"And what about my husband and the business, then?" she exclaimed, with indignation.

"Oh—that! A great advertisement, Mrs Findlater. You'll have all London flocking here for its cabbages. And when you're released—think of it!—the public sympathy and indignation. Why, it's a fortune, Mrs Findlater. Now—I must go. Can I take it you say nothing about Julep or anybody else? You will remember, won't you? I would simply love to hear you ticking off my friend Grainger, but I can't stay."

Mr Pinson looked hard at her.

"All right," she said. "You seem straight. I'll say nothing."

"You may be sure," said Mr Pinson, backing out of the room, "that silence is golden, Mrs Findlater. Goodbye. I shall see you again, no doubt."

Mr Pinson's next order to his taxi-driver was the Adelphi, where he kept him long enough to collect a suitcase full of belongings; and he dismissed him at last at Victoria Station.

The next morning Mr Pinson was in Paris and installed once more at the Hôtel Edouard Sept. On this occasion the purlieus of the Marché St Honoré had no immediate attraction for him. Having bathed and shaved and breakfasted, Mr Pinson betook himself straightway to the Prefect of Police.

No, he said, in answer to inquiries at the Prefecture, he had no appointment with Monsieur L, but he had a letter which he begged might be handed to Monsieur at once. And he took from his letter-case an envelope addressed to the Prefect, bearing on its back a stamp which at once evoked respect and promptitude. Within five minutes Mr Pinson was shown into the great man's room.

"You bring a letter from a friend of mine, Monsieur Pinson," said he, glancing at it. "Sir Arthur asks me to do anything I can for you. Now, tell me the affair."

He pointed to a chair and himself stood leaning against the mantelpiece.

"I hardly dare trouble you personally, monsieur," said Mr Pinson. "I was hoping you might instruct some reliable member of your staff——"

"No no, not at all," he said. "Sir Arthur would not have written for nothing. I wish to know everything. Tell me, if you please."

"It will be long," said Mr Pinson.

"Not too long. There is a day before us," he replied with a ceremonial bow. "Monsieur is an advocate, I gather. He has some delicate affair in hand. We can help. Good. Now!"

Mr Pinson inclined his head.

"I will be as short as possible," he said. "A criminal case has occurred in England in which a friend of mine is involved. He has been indiscreet but perfectly innocent. I wish to extricate him."

Thus Mr Pinson launched into an explanation of the facts about Westmore Colebroke's disappearance, his antecedents, and the discoveries that had been made at Longbridge. At intervals the Prefect touched a button and whispered to the messenger who answered, and duly received two or three dossiers of papers.

When the whole case had been unfolded to him, he looked through these documents, selected a certain number, and sat down with them at his table.

"Voilà!" said he. "It is very clever. You should have been in the Sureté, Monsieur Pinson, and not at the bar."

"You flatter me," replied Mr Pinson.

"Not a bit," said the Prefect. "Now where are we? You do not believe that the body found in the coffre-fort was the body of Mr Westmore Colebroke, hein? Well, it was not. Mr Westmore Colebroke was in Paris up to last week. Since which we have lost sight of him."

"Which day last week?" asked Mr Pinson.

"Last Saturday night."

"The night I was shadowed at the hotel!" Mr Pinson reflected.

"Yes, monsieur. We have a perfect record of Mr Colebroke until you appear on the scene, and then—zut!—he is gone. You seem to have frightened him away."

"Or," said Mr Pinson, "I may have frightened some other people. Colebroke did not know me. My presence would not have alarmed him. It is now several days since the reports of his murder were published. Why has he not appeared to announce that he is not murdered?"

"You suggest," said the Prefect, "that there are people who have an interest in his concealment?"

"I suggest that it is possible. I hesitate to put my feeble theories before an expert like monsieur——"

"Là, là! We can do without compliments, monsieur. Tell me! I listen. You have a theory?"

"Yes, and it has worked so far. It is this: When Colebroke came back to England from Paris he found on the quays of Westport a man whom he had just known in his student days as an habitué of the Brasserie Boucher—Lebaudy. They renewed acquaintance. Colebroke loved Paris and loved to talk over Paris days with Lebaudy, though he was only a potato merchant in a small way of business. When Moreau came out of prison, he vowed vengeance on Colebroke. He seemed to have some muddy notion that Colebroke was responsible for his sufferings. When Moreau left France for England and went to Longbridge, it could only have been for the purpose of carrying out his scheme of revenge. Obviously somebody warned Colebroke. I imagine it was Lebaudy."

The Prefect nodded his head as Mr Pinson made his points.

"Colebroke resolved that he would disappear in order to baulk Moreau of his chance. Why he did this I have not been able to guess. It would have been so much simpler to put the matter in the hands of the police and let them deal with Monsieur Moreau. But he did it, and some day no doubt we shall discover the reason. Now, monsieur, Colebroke was only just in time. The very night he vanished an attack was made on his house—and I have no doubt made by Moreau or by somebody on his behalf. I myself saw the bullet-mark upon the blind of Colebroke's office. The police think the shots were fired inside the room. I have no doubt they were fired from outside. But Colebroke escaped. He came to Paris—no doubt because he knew that Moreau dared not re-enter France. Colebroke had good friends in Paris. I think Papa Boucher was one; certainly the gentleman who kidnapped me in London, M Laroche, was another. By the way, do you know of Monsieur Laroche?"

"No," said the Prefect, "not as Monsieur Laroche. But I think I can identify that monsieur as Monsieur Philippe de la Roche d'Arvor—an excellent friend of mine, though a little wild in his politics. It is very likely. But go on, Monsieur Pinson."

"Colebroke came to Paris. Clearly he was in some sort of communication with Miss Elburton, who knew of his danger but never for a moment believed the story of his death. Possibly through Lebaudy. I think that was it. Now, monsieur, no sooner do I come to Paris than the friends of Colebroke leap to the conclusion that I am an agent of Moreau and seeking to injure Colebroke. Then apparently they chase me to London, and Colebroke himself vanishes again. Colebroke is an Englishman. He must know of the things that have happened in Longbridge. It is imperative that he should now appear. But where is he?"

"Ah, where he is? My dear Monsieur Pinson," said the Prefect, "I see you have a theory. Tell me still."

"I argue from character, monsieur. I may be wrong, but I think I am right. Colebroke is an Englishman and a lawyer. He knows how imperative it is, as I say, that he should now appear to clear up this mystery. If he were able to do so, he would, at any risk to himself. The deduction is that he is not able to do so. He is, in fact being detained by force."

"Ah!" exclaimed the Prefect. "By whom? You still have a theory? Continue."

"By Moreau or by agents of Moreau."

"But—Moreau is in England. Moreau dare not enter France!"

"I am sorry, Monsieur le Préfet, to appear to contradict you," said Mr Pinson, "but I think Moreau is in France, and I believe unknown to the friends of Colebroke. Monsieur Laroche clearly thought Moreau was at Longbridge. But when my detective friend Grainger, of whom I have spoken, broke into the house where Moreau was supposed to be, he found only a man passing as Victor Leduc, who could not have been Moreau since he was addressed by the woman as Victor and not as Antoine. Therefore he is Victor somebody-or-other. Moreau knew that Colebroke had escaped him. Don't you think——"

"A moment, monsieur," said the Prefect, turning over the sheets of one of his files. "Victor—Victor Un-tel . . . Who can it be? . . . Ah, yes. Possibly . . . There was a Victor Lemaître. Possibly."

His dark eyes looked keenly into Pinson's.

"So, you think . . . But how could Moreau get through the ports? It would be difficult."

"With respect," said Mr Pinson, "it may not be quite so difficult as it looks. Of course, I hesitate, as a mere amateur, to make a suggestion. But——"

"Go on, my good sir," the Prefect said; "let us get out all that is in our minds."

"Very well. I have with me a dossier of documents—the correspondence which was . . . discovered"—Mr Pinson smiled as he searched for the word—"discovered for me at the house where Mr Leduc resides, or resided, at Longbridge."

"Ah!" The eyes of Monsieur le Préfet gleamed as Mr Pinson drew from his pocket a packet of papers.

"These are rough translations by a friend of mine of the letters which he . . . discovered. They relate chiefly to the affairs of some League, and I have no doubt they will be very interesting to your department when there is leisure to examine them. But I know nothing about the League, and that part of the matter has no concern for me. It is only to one letter that I wish to draw your attention—a letter from Paris written a fortnight ago. This is it."

Mr Pinson selected a paper in Grainger's laborious handwriting, and laid it on the table.

"This," said he, "is how my friend has translated it:

Paris, June —.

One could arrange a rendezvous NDS if you would send a telegram sufficiently able asking him to meet L at M on June —.

The Prefect was puzzled by this English.

"Can we get it back into French?" he asked.

"Nearly enough, I think," said Mr Pinson. "My friend has evidently got it literally enough, but I imagine that it would be clearer if you translated *habile* as 'clever' instead of 'able'."

"'A telegram sufficiently clever,'" mused the Prefect. "Ah—un piège!—a trap."

"Exactly," said Mr Pinson. "A forged telegram to him—that is, Colebroke. From L—that is Lebaudy. At M—that is where I break down, and also at NDS. I thought, with much deference, Monsieur le Préfet, that in the archives of the Posts and Telegraphs——"

But the Prefect had already pressed a button, and a silent clerk was standing beside him, to whom he gave rapid instructions, ending, "Dans cinq minutes, pas plus, voyez!"

"In five minutes, Mr Pinson, we shall know. You are to be felicitated; it is a very good deduction. In the meantime, if I may suggest it to you, shall we get my friend M de la Roche d'Arvor to meet us? I think he would be of some use."

"I should be delighted to meet Mr Laroche again," said Mr Pinson, "and renew my apologies for the discourtesies of our last encounter."

"Then if you will excuse me, I will telephone to him. Will you smoke a cigarette?"

Mr Pinson sat back in his chair while the Prefect secured a call and talked into the telephone receiver. Before the conversation was finished, the silent clerk was standing at his elbow again. The Prefect took from him the paper he held, and read.

"Mr Pinson," he said, when the messenger had retired, "we have it! A telegram signed by Lebaudy was handed in at Westport on June —, addressed not to Colebroke but to de la Roche d'Arvor. Here it is: 'Ask C to reach Morlaix station by night train 27th. Urgent. Lebaudy.'"

"Morlaix!" Mr Pinson exclaimed. "We have it indeed, monsieur! There is a small packet-boat which runs from Westport to the Brittany ports and calls at Morlaix once a week in the summer. Lebaudy doubtless does business by it. That was a clever telegram, eh?"

"Yes—but it was not very clever to send it to M de la Roche d'Arvor, eh?"

"I have been wondering," said Mr Pinson, "why you suggested immediately, and before you knew of this, that we should see M de la Roche d'Arvor."

"Oh, simply because I knew that he and Mr Colebroke were close friends. But this is a touch of luck. Already we can translate the letter completely with the exception of the letters 'NDS' I rely on M d'Arvor for that. He is a Breton—and that is the only excuse for his deplorable politics. He will be here as soon as his auto can bring him."

And within a quarter of an hour, Mr Pinson was shaking hands again with the gentleman whose hospitality he had enjoyed under such remarkable circumstances in London.

"We have been at cross purposes, monsieur," said Mr Pinson, when the Prefect had made a sketchy explanation of the meeting. "You thought I was an agent of Moreau, and I thought you were an agent of Moreau. You were a friend of Colebroke's and I thought you his enemy. I was a friend of Colebroke's and you thought I was his enemy. Is it not so?"

"Precisely," said M d'Arvor. "But in the presence of Monsieur le Préfet, as he well understands," and they bowed to each other, "I can enter into no explanations of my connection with Mr Colebroke or of his connection with me, or of the circumstances under which we have both become involved in the follies of that imbecile Moreau. That is a political matter, hein? We do not discuss it."

"Let us say, my dear sir, that I know nothing about it," said the Prefect, with a smile. "The important thing is to elucidate this letter and discover the trap into which Mr Colebroke has been drawn. You are a Breton. You know the Morlaix country. Can you translate for us 'NDS'?"

"Without doubt. But first I want to have some idea of Mr Pinson's position. How much does he know of this affair?"

The Prefect looked to Mr Pinson with an interrogation.

"I will tell you shortly all I know," said he. "Of the politics of it, nothing."

"This letter——" M d'Arvor pointed to Grainger's scrawl.

"I came into possession of it by . . . an accident," said Mr Pinson. "My interest in the affair is that I am the representative of Colebroke's closest friend in England, the father of his fiancée. The Moreau affair caused Colebroke to disappear, and his disappearance, for reasons which I need not now explain, caused great embarrassment to his friend. I undertook to discover him, and soon came to the conclusion that he was in Paris. But my inquiries revealed a shocking murder in Longbridge, where he lived, and the body was wrongly identified as Colebroke's. I knew he was not dead; but a man's neck was in danger because of his supposed death. Second reason for discovering Colebroke. This letter shows clearly enough that Colebroke himself has been trapped into danger. Third reason for discovering him. The telegram you received was sent by people who knew of Lebaudy's association with Colebroke, and I have no doubt in my own mind that they had discovered or divined an arrangement made by Colebroke with his fiancée to communicate with him through Lebaudy if there was any urgency to do so——"

"Ah!" cried M d'Arvor. "That explains——"

"What?" said Mr Pinson and the Prefect in unison.

"Colebroke's immense agitation when the telegram came. I never saw a man in so great a state of excitement. He rushed off and took the train to Morlaix within the hour."

"And," said Mr Pinson, "you have not seen him since?"

"No."

"Nor heard of him?"

"Not a word. I have been expecting him every day to return."

"Excuse me, monsieur," said the Prefect, looking at his watch. "But you have not yet translated for us the mysterious letters 'NDS'."

Undoubtedly they stand for 'Nôtre Dame de Secours,'" said M La Roche,

"Which means——"

"Nôtre Dame de Secours is a tiny hamlet in the forest near the Morlaix coast, about twenty kilometres from the town. I know it well."

"And can you suggest any reason for a rendezvous at Nôtre Dame de Secours?"

"None whatever, unless it were a rendezvous intended to be kept in absolute secrecy. You might search France all over and not find a more obscure or secluded spot."

The Prefect looked at his watch again.

"Messieurs," said he, "the Brest express leaves the Invalides at midday and reaches Morlaix at eleven o'clock. It is now half an hour to noon. I suggest that you should call a taxi-auto without delay. Two agents will be ready to accompany you. I will telegraph for a reliable auto to meet you at Morlaix. I draw your attention to the fact that the rendezvous was for four days ago, and many thing can happen in four days in the loneliest spot in France."

IX

The State Railway of France did its best with the long and curly route from Paris to the Far West. It was really a very good best. The midday express got along at a respectable pace and did not make too many stops.

But for the two men who sat in a first-class compartment undisturbed, who were eyed with profound respect by the railway officials because of the two agents of the Sureté who in a nearby compartment guarded them, no train could have gone fast enough and every stop was too much.

Mr Pinson, having at first taken a light and airy view of the situation, gradually dropped the note of blague. M d'Arvor knew a great deal about this affair of which Mr Pinson had been in ignorance, and as he communicated his information so at the same time he communicated his fears to his companion.

Mr Pinson had been unable to understand how Colebroke's attitude at the trial of Antoine Moreau could have inspired that rabid politician with so intense a hatred.

"The evidence at the trial!" said M d'Arvor. "Phut! The evidence at the trial had nothing whatever to do with it. Colebroke was an Englishman who had no concern whatever with our League. How could he? His evidence about the meeting was a bagatelle. The police would have got Moreau convicted anyhow. Search deeper, my friend. Search where one should always search—seek the woman!"

"Oh!" exclaimed Mr Pinson. "So there was a woman?"

"Of course. It is a vendetta. Moreau is mad. He is murderous."

M d'Arvor looked impatiently at the flying landscape and fidgeted his fingers upon the window-pane.

"I feel a great responsibility, Monsieur," he said, "for it was I who got Colebroke into this tangle. But for me he would never have known Moreau. We were close friends for years. I was very fond of Colebroke. He is a fine type—quite English, but broader in his interests than the English are ordinarily—pardon me. A lawyer, yes—but also an artist. Moreau also—an artist, a musician, without doubt. You know the sort of society that one keeps in Paris when one is a Bohemian. It was the League that brought me into association with Moreau, but it was art that mixed us all."

"Including the woman?" Mr Pinson asked.

"Yes, the woman included. You remember that at the trial there was mentioned a lady—an English lady, Miss Vincent—who was the *amie* of Antoine Moreau?"

Mr Pinson recalled the name from the files of the newspaper.

"That is the woman. Moreau was infatuated with her. She had dropped down in Paris from the sky after the War. A very beautiful girl. Said to be of a respectable English family. But she has no importance in this except her reaction on Colebroke. You know that extraordinary man——"

"No," said Mr Pinson. "You forget I have never seen him, and had hardly heard of him till a fortnight ago."

"Ah well! Colebroke, then, is an extraordinary man. He is what you call a Puritan, I think. He has the most fastidious ideas about women. They are sacred creatures to him. He surrounds them with an atmosphere of mystery and holiness—mon dieu! I suppose it is because he does not know them. And of all the women in the world, naturally for Colebroke the most holy and the most mysterious are Englishwomen. An English girl must not be touched, she must hardly be thought about—she must be spoken of in whispers. What Frenchmen do with their own women is their own affair. But an English girl—là, là! So that when Colebroke heard of Moreau's liaison with Miss Vincent..."

"I suppose he went off the deep end," said Mr Pinson.

"You would say?"

"Sorry. That's slang—*de l'argot*: my vice. He was enraged?"

"Precisely: he was enraged. He was Don Quixote. He would not meet Moreau. But he sought the girl. It seemed that he had known something of her: she had nursed him in a hospital when he was wounded at the beginning of the War. She had talked to him of her home and her family in England."

"Young?" asked Mr Pinson.

"Yes, not much more than what you call a 'flapper.' Very young. The idea of her association with Moreau roused Monsieur le Puritan to fury. He worked and argued and pleaded and persuaded her to end it. He communicated with her family, and just before the arrest she broke with Moreau. Unfortunately it was too late, and she also was arrested. Colebroke stayed in Paris after the trial specially to watch her interests. He got her father over to take her back to England."

"It may all seem very eccentric, but it does not provide a plausible reason why Moreau should hate Colebroke at the point of the revolver," said Mr Pinson.

"That, my dear monsieur, is because you do not know Moreau. Moreau is the type of passionate man who could not possibly believe that Colebroke acted from disinterested motives. He could not conceive the existence of a Puritan—no! What Moreau believed was that Colebroke had stolen his *amie* because he wanted her for himself. That is what Moreau believes now. He is mad—mad with passion, jealousy, revenge. He would kill both

Colebroke and the girl if he could find them. When I heard after his release that he had gone to England, I warned my friend Colebroke, and you know what precautions he took to avoid the vengeance. He came to me at once. I asked him why he had not taken the plain course and sought the protection of the English police. What do you think his reason was?"

"It is the one thing I have not been able to understand," said Mr Pinson.

"A mad reason, monsieur! Yet I love him for it. Don Quixote again. When Miss Vincent went back to England, all the Paris adventure was hidden. Nobody knew anything of it. Being a very beautiful young girl and of a well-placed family, she soon married. Don Quixote rejoiced in this end of the affair. In the meantime, he himself was in love with your Miss Elburton. A charming girl—not beautiful, but very interesting, very good ——"

"You know her!" exclaimed Mr Pinson.

"No—not yet. But Colebroke has shown to me her portrait. She will spend her honeymoon in France, if—— Ah, how slow this sacré train!"

"Colebroke has told you of her?"

"Oh, much, much! He can talk of nothing else, the Puritan lover! When he received my warning about Moreau and took his Quixotic decision, he told the whole story to Miss Elburton. No doubt she thought it was a very fine story of which Colebroke was the shining hero. No doubt. And he swore her to be secret about it. She was not to speak a word, whatever happened. And of course she did not speak."

"Not a single word," said Mr Pinson. "Only her eyes and her blushes spoke for her."

"Ah yes: she has serious eyes, eloquent eyes," said M d'Arvor. "Colebroke has told me about them. Also about her broad brow and her gentle voice, and her wit, and her piano-playing, and her garden, and the way she walks, and his worship of her purity and excellence. My dear Monsieur Pinson—I have heard it all a hundred times in three months. The only thing I have not heard is what she says to him in her letters."

"Letters? She wrote to him?"

"Oh yes, and he to her—through his friend Lebaudy. That is why, when the false telegram came from Lebaudy, he immediately jumped at the thought that something was wrong, some trouble for Miss Elburton. I tell you, he was like a maniac. And he has fallen into a trap—Colebroke is in a foolish trap!"

M d'Arvor tapped the window, got up, walked the length of the carriage, and sat down again, cursing the train, and the Government's railway administration, and its engines, and the stations at which they stopped.

The train rolled on westward through the day and into the evening. They lunched. They smoked and pretended to read. They dined. But always they returned to the discussion of Colebroke's fate.

"One thing I have not grasped," Mr Pinson said, as they returned to their seats after dinner. "It is what Colebroke intended to do ultimately. How long did he mean to let Mr Moreau hold him up if the discovery at Longbridge had not come to put an end to the business?"

"Until Moreau was arrested again—and he thought, quite properly, that would not be very long. Moreau in England could not be touched without raising the episode of Miss Vincent. But Moreau had been exiled from France, and as soon as he entered the country he would be arrested with no question of Miss Vincent. We were trying all the time to lure him into France. We even had anonymous letters sent from Paris to Moreau informing him where Colebroke was to be found and suggesting ways of getting into the country without being seen. But they produced nothing. Moreau was afraid, suspicious—or so we thought. He smelt the police in that. But now it is all clear, is it not?"

"I don't quite see——" Mr Pinson began.

"Ah, Monsieur Pinson, your perspicuity is so great that you must see. When Lebaudy warned us about your inquiries, we thought we had him—that he was about to strike. We shadowed you—and we went off on a false scent. But now—cannot you see why Moreau did not come? We knew nothing about the attack he made on Colebroke's house. It is clear that Moreau thought he had killed Colebroke, and fled to some other part of England, and he left that rascal Lemaître in Longbridge to watch how things went."

Mr Pinson shook his head, and blew cigarette smoke for several minutes.

"Do you say," he asked at last, "that Colebroke did not know an attack had been made, and that there had been shooting?"

"No—and nobody else knew, apparently, until the body was found. At least, that is what you tell me. I did not myself know it when I was in London."

"Then," said Mr Pinson, "what exactly did Colebroke do after he left the Elburtons' house that night?"

M d'Arvor shrugged his shoulders.

"I don't know. You see, there was no particular interest in the point. Colebroke told me that he left England suddenly on receiving my warning. That is all."

"Of course," said Mr Pinson. "And Colebroke doesn't even now know that he's supposed to be dead, and that the whole country is in an uproar about it?"

"Not the least in the world," M d'Arvor replied.

Mr Pinson consumed another cigarette, leaning back with his eyes closed.

"Julep!" he said, when he opened them again, "I thought you an honest man, but you're evidently a thief."

"*Comment?*" said M d'Arvor, startled.

"Oh, nothing," said Mr Pinson. "I was only thinking aloud."

X

Eleven o'clock at night. The *rapide* slowed down over the vast granite viaduct spanning with its two tiers of arches the steep valley at Morlaix, and pulled up in the station. A few lights twinkled in the darkness below, but the venerable city was asleep, the station almost deserted.

D'Arvor and Mr Pinson, descending, found the two agents already alighted. Following them to the rear of the train and across the tracks to the exit, they saw beyond the barrier a big car waiting, engine running. A porter or two hovered by.

The agents spoke a few words to the chauffeur and indicated to him M d'Arvor.

"To Plestin, as fast as you can drive," said M d'Arvor.

The four men entered the car. On the heights above Morlaix the June night was clear; but within a few kilomètres they ran into a thin mist, which reduced their speed. As they drew nearer to the coast the mist thickened into a sea fog, and the car's pace was perforce brought down to a crawl. The driver groped his way into a wall of white cloud lit by his headlights.

M d'Arvor peered out, scanning the roadside when it could be discerned. He knew the road well, he said, and it was fairly simple; but in such a murk there was always the possibility of going wrong.

At the end of the half hour which should have brought them to the little town of Plestin, the driver had to confess himself at fault. He crawled on till the blurred light showed a roadside house.

M d'Arvor stopped him and got out. The blue and white walls of a large building could be dimly seen. M d'Arvor hammered at the door and looked to the upper windows for an answering gleam of light. But it was from the doorway itself that the answer came. An old man holding a lamp in his hand opened to the summons.

"We have lost our way," said M d'Arvor. "We want the road to Plestin."

The old man raised the lamp and peered into the speaker's face.

"You are having a game with me, Monsieur Lucien," said he. "What brings you out at this time of night?"

"Eh!" cried M d'Arvor. "But it's Marnier! And this—is this the Buisson d'Or? What a fool I am! I give you my faith, Père Marnier, that we lost our way in the fog, and thought we were off the road—and I never recognised the Buisson d'Or."

"Are we all right?" asked Mr Pinson from the car.

"Yes—on the high road," replied M d'Arvor, "but a long way from Plestin yet."

"Will you enter, messieurs?" the old man inquired.

"No, we are in a hurry. How long have you had this fog?"

"Three days, Monsieur Lucien. But not so thick as this. They say it has been very bad in the Channel. You have come from Morlaix?"

"Yes."

"The others came from Locquirec, and they had it just as bad," said the innkeeper.

"The others? What others?"

"There were two messieurs and a dame in a car from Locquirec, trying to find their way to Plestin—about half an hour ago. At least I suppose it was Plestin, though they were going the wrong way. And they continued to go the wrong way. You are going to visit your uncle. Monsieur Lucien?"

"Probably tomorrow," M d'Arvor answered. "Pardon, Père Marnier, for disturbing you—and goodnight. Now we know where we are, we will go back to Morlaix and not try to reach Plestin tonight."

He instructed the driver to turn the car and drive slowly up the hill.

"Here," said he to Mr Pinson, "I am in my native country—and I should never have thought a fog would prevent me from recognising it. That's an old inn where I have stayed a hundred times when fishing in the River Douron. But most important of all—we are quite close to our destination."

"Ah!" said Mr Pinson. "So we did not want to go to Plestin?"

"No. Plestin was for the benefit of the railway officials at Morlaix."

Half way up the long hill, M d'Arvor stopped the car.

"It is necessary to decide exactly how we shall all act," he said. "You gentlemen are armed, without doubt?"

The two officers were certainly armed. They tapped the pockets where their automatics were concealed.

"I hope you will have no need to use those things," said M d'Arvor. "You understood from the Prefect how the affair stands —that if our suspicions are correct we shall find Antoine Moreau here and in a desperate mood? Very well. The place to which I am going to take you is two kilomètres through the woods, by a narrow lane which leaves the road just above this. At the bottom of the valley is a small farm house which has been used as a rendezvous by myself and certain friends. On what we find there depends our course of action. But I wish you two gentlemen to remain out of sight entirely until we need your help. I can appear there without creating any suspicion. Monsieur Pinson is unknown to anybody, and will be guaranteed by me. It is only in case of violence that we shall want you. Therefore, when the car stops where I shall direct, remain by it and see what happens."

The car was turned into the narrow by-way. M d'Arvor ordered the lights to be switched off, and the steep lane through the woods was slowly negotiated. The mist was thick as ever, and, as they descended into a deep gorge, it became impenetrable to the eye.

They stopped at a point where the declivity flattened out.

M d'Arvor invited Mr Pinson to accompany him, and told the two agents to stay with the car while they reconnoitred. He had his suspicions about the two gentlemen and the lady who had been motoring past the Buisson d'Or at that time of night. He did not want to stumble on them accidentally.

"We will go through the wood just here. It is not two hundred mètres to the farm, and we can see whether a car has arrived there. We shall come out in a grassy avenue that leads from the farm up the hill to the Chapel of Nôtre Dame de Secours. Follow me, Mr Pinson."

The two men entered the wood by a little track, feeling their way cautiously through the fog.

Mr Pinson, who had followed close upon the heels of M d'Arvor, stepping silently, suddenly felt a sharp blow on his head and went down like a chopped log. It was so sudden that he did not even cry out, and so violent that he was stunned for a few moments. Recovering, he lay still, expecting to be attacked again or seized. But nothing moved. There was no sound in the woods. M d'Arvor's footsteps were out of hearing.

He could not understand what had happened till he rose cautiously and found his head and shoulders in a thick growth of leaves and twigs, dripping with moisture, and feeling about, touched a stout branch immediately in front of his face.

Then Mr Pinson, in spite of his hurt, smiled to himself. It was the low growing branch of a tree that had attacked him. In the darkness he had lost M d'Arvor's track and wandered away from the path into the wood itself. The most amusing part of the incident was that in his fall he had lost all sense of direction, and stood with his head in the foliage uncertain which way to go.

And there Mr Pinson would have stood, waiting till d'Arvor missed him and came back to search for him, if he had not suddenly heard voices. They came to his ears full and plump, without warning, and from not far away. He could even make out that two men were talking in French.

His first impulse was to start off in the direction from which the sound seemed to come. His second to listen a moment more.

The voices approached. They sounded loud in the stillness. He even heard two words distinctly. But there were no footsteps. The voices seemed to pass him within a few yards and then to fade away.

Mr Pinson hesitated a few seconds and felt his hip-pocket; then he said to himself, "Well, Pinson—here goes! Our friend d'Arvor has missed them. It's up to you."

He was now in no doubt about direction. Extending his hands in front of him, he pushed his way through the thin undergrowth of the wood in something as near a straight line as possible, and within twenty yards burst into the open. It was open in the sense that a perceptible brightening of the fog betokened sky above, and his feet were on turf.

Mr Pinson stopped and listened intently. . . . Nothing.

Then a distant note, muffled by the fog. It was a woman's voice, very faint, away on his left. He crept towards it, still stretching out his hands, and after twenty paces stopped again to listen.

"Victor! Tu y es?"

The voice was at his ear almost.

Mr Pinson's brain worked rapidly. It flew back to Longbridge and the house by the river that Grainger had described to him. It speculated for a fraction of a second whether he should answer the question. It rejected that plan. And in less than five seconds Mr Pinson was grateful to it.

In those five seconds three things happened. Mr Pinson, stretching hands and feeling round in the fog, touched something smooth and wet and hard. A blur of light almost blinded him. A man's voice said, "Ah, nous y sommes!"

Mr Pinson stepped back a pace, and the light which had so suddenly shone into the fog became dull. Another pace, and he could see it no longer. But the voices were plain enough. A rapid conversation followed. Mr Pinson listened to it breathlessly. It gave him the information he wanted.

It told him where he was. The turf under his feet was the floor of the grass-grown avenue d'Arvor had described.

The smooth hard surface he had touched was the tonneau of the car that had been seen by Père Marnier.

The lady in the car was the Madame Leduc to whom Grainger had restored a packet of letters at Longbridge.

The man who spoke to her was the gentleman who called himself Victor Leduc.

The silent and invisible auditor of this conversation listened painfully, hardly daring to breathe. For it told him exactly what Messieurs Moreau and Leduc intended to do, and what he must do if he would circumvent their pleasant purpose. The last sentences Mr Pinson heard were these:

"I am afraid, Victor! I do not like it."

"There is nothing to fear, mignonne. Antoine will be here in ten minutes. He has gone to make some arrangements with Yves at the farm. He will tell you what to do. Have no fear."

Mr Pinson advanced till he caught the white glow in the fog from the light which M Victor Leduc probably held in his hand—an electric torch, very likely. Mr Pinson skirted the light, walking silently on the grass. The ground rose before him. He went on and upward, still with hands outstretched.

He had ten minutes. They would be enough if only he could be sure that he would not walk again into the wood, and if luck held. The fog that made him go so slowly was a nuisance; but it was also a nuisance to his friends the enemy. It worked both ways.

Up—always up! The grassy road was steep. And as he went, Mr Pinson's heart grew lighter, for the fog lessened. He caught a glimpse of great boles on his right hand—first one, then another, and they gave him a line. He sharpened his pace. He walked with confidence. He had no longer to grope with outstretched hands.

Presently a thin mist was all that hindered him. There was light in the summer sky. Against it a dark mass heaved up in front of him. He climbed a short flight of granite steps. He crossed an open forecourt. He stood under a pointed arch. He knocked hard upon a huge door, and waited.

"Qui va là?" said a voice from the other side of the door.

"Colebroke! Is that you?" asked Mr Pinson.

"Who is that speaking English?" said the voice.

"Colebroke, for heaven's sake believe me," said Mr Pinson. "You are in a ghastly trap. There's only ten minutes for everything. Can you get out of the beastly place?"

"Who are you?" said the voice.

"You wouldn't know me," said Mr Pinson. "But I'm an Englishman and a lawyer, and I represent your friend Elburton."

There was a noise of unbolting. The door moved back.

"I'm armed," said the voice. "Are you alone?"

"Absolutely," replied Mr Pinson.

"Then come in," said the voice.

Mr Pinson entered. The door closed behind him and was bolted again.

XI

Within five minutes Mr Pinson was the sole tenant of the neglected votive Chapelle de Nôtre Dame de Secours, except the owls that fidgeted in corners of the broken walls and the mice that scampered over the floor. There was light enough for him to make out the outlines of pointed windows, but not enough to enable him to move with confidence. So he just stood by the door.

If there had been adequate light, the owls and the mice would have been able to see a smile on the face of Mr Pinson. He had recovered his aplomb and attained the light-comedy mood again. He waited for the curtain to ring up.

The ring came when he heard a rustle of footsteps on the grass of the forecourt and a light tapping at the door.

"Hullo!" said Mr Pinson, in his cheeriest English tones and as loud as he could shout. "Who's there?"

His voice echoed round the hollow of the chapel like a thunderstorm. There was a squealing and skittering of birds and animals.

"Westmore!" The voice was a woman's and not raised much above a whisper.

"Ye gods!" yelled Mr Pinson. "Who's that? It can't be——"

"Westmore!" said the voice. "Speak not so loud. There is danger. Open. Let me in!"

"Is that you, Maud, my darling?" Mr Pinson inquired in more moderate tones.

"Yes, Westmore, it is I. Let me in."

Mr Pinson loosened his necktie and took it off.

"In one moment, darling," he said.

Very deliberately he slid back the bolts, took the huge key from the door, and slipped it into his pocket. He pulled the door open an inch or two and stood behind it.

The lady pressed upon the door, pushed it back, and advanced groping with her hands in front of her face.

"Darling!" cried Mr Pinson as he seized her by the waist, slipped the noose he had made with the necktie over her head, and pulled it tight in a perfectly effective gag. She had not uttered a sound.

Mr Pinson swung the door home and closed it with a single bolt. He then addressed the lady.

"Madame, I hold in my hand an automatic pistol which will be used with absolute precision unless you do exactly what I tell you, and do it without hesitation. You understand English well enough to follow me, I think. I have reason to suppose you are not in this plot of your own free will. Possibly you meant to warn me a moment ago. If that is so, you can indicate it by tapping my arm. . . .

"Very well. Now are you prepared to obey my instructions? Good. I shall not ungag you, but I will give you a chance. Two men will be here in a minute. You will admit them. The instant you have admitted them, you will get outside. After that, sauve qui peut. I cannot help what becomes of you. Is it understood? Then . . . attention!"

Standing behind the door with his hand grasping the woman's arm, Mr Pinson waited.

Again the rustling of the grass in the forecourt. Again the knock on the door.

"Miss Elburton!" came in a hoarse whisper.

Mr Pinson pulled the woman towards the door; he even slid back the bolt for her. Two shadows passed in. In an instant Pinson had bundled the woman out, followed her, and pulled the door after him. The key was turned in the lock.

"Allez!" said Mr Pinson. The woman's figure vanished into the mist.

The two men left in the chapel apparently did not at first realise what had happened during those five seconds, for there was no sound of disturbance. Then Mr Pinson, standing guard over the door, saw a bright light flash up inside as an electric torch was lit, and heard a loud curse. He smiled grimly and kept his eyes directed down the avenue and his ears open for the voices he awaited.

They came at last—a murmur in the distance. Then he heard the thud of running feet upon the grass. Presently, four men were rushing up the granite steps and across the forecourt.

Mr Pinson stepped out to meet them.

A light was flashed on him. "Thank God, my friend!" cried M d'Arvor. "You are safe. And those others?"

Mr Pinson indicated the building behind him.

"Caught in their own trap," said he, showing the key turned in the lock upon them.

"Splendid!" said M d'Arvor. "But——"

He ran from the group around the chapel to the south-east.

Mr Pinson had a sense of fatality—a succession of prickly heats and frozen sweats while M d'Arvor was absent. He came back, not running, but trailing his feet.

"It is too bad, my friend," said he, "but you could not of course know it. They were easily able to get away by the little door of the oratory."

Mr Pinson exploded a word. Then he cried, "The car!"

"Listen!" said one of the agents.

And in the bottom of the valley they heard a dull note which rose to a shriek as a car in low gear tore up the hill on the other side.

"Never mind," said M d'Arvor. "Here is Colebroke, safe and sound."

"Yes," remarked the young man with a beard who stood by his side, "and I should like to shake hands with Mr Pinson."

XII

It was two o'clock in the morning when Mr Pinson was allowed to prepare for bed. No bright ornament of the English bar, he felt sure, had ever prepared to go to bed in a more extraordinary place or in a more remarkable fashion.

After the trapped birds had broken silently out of the trap, and the sound of the screaming gears had died away, the five men gathered in the forecourt of the Chapelle Nôtre Dame de Secours had remained gloomily silent for a few moments.

Then Mr Pinson yawned.

M d'Arvor laughed sympathetically. Well, he said, there was nothing to be done. Unless messieurs les agents...

The two emissaries of the Prefect conferred. They seemed to be in some difficulty. If they could have the car, they might be able to run down the fugitives. But M d'Arvor and his friends would doubtless want the car to return to Morlaix.

Then M d'Arvor yawned.

Suddenly an idea occurred to him.

"Colebroke," he said, "we are all sleepy. Let us command beds of Yves down there. Messieurs les agents can have the car. We will find our own way back tomorrow. What do you think?"

They all moved down the grassy avenue. At the bottom, the agents disappeared into the fog to make their arrangements with the chauffeur. M d'Arvor took the arms of his two companions, and led them a few steps, through a wide gateway, across a dusty farmyard, pushed open a door, and ushered them into a huge low room lit by a hanging lamp. Mr Pinson had not previously seen the interior of a Breton farmhouse. He looked with surprise at its floor of mud caked hard, its black rafters with festoons of dried meats depending, its vast hearth with seats in the very chimney place itself, and a tripod suspending a crock over the embers of a wood fire; but with most astonishment at the row of elaborately decorated wood panels covering two of the walls.

As they entered, a tall dark man in blouse and coarse trousers rose from the chimney corner and started forward as from a shock. Then, seeing M d'Arvor, he stood still and saluted respectfully.

"Ah—Monsieur Lucien!" he said.

"Salut, Yves," said M d'Arvor.

M d'Arvor plunged into a rapid conversation with the tall man in a clattering language of which Mr Pinson could not understand a word. M d'Arvor became excited, angry, and appeased in turn; the tall man gesticulated, pointed to the wooden panels, shrugged his shoulders, and pleaded.

The argument was witnessed by Mr Pinson with watchful eyes. He could not understand a word of the dialogue, but the features of Monsieur Yves and his expression as he countered everything that M d'Arvor said interested Mr Pinson keenly.

At length M d'Arvor turned to his two friends.

"Yves, here, is making difficulty," he said. "He does not want our company. I tell him that he has put us to so much inconvenience by his folly in assisting Moreau—though he knew nothing about it—that the least he can do is to give us three of his *lits closes* till the morning."

"I suppose," said Mr Pinson, "there is not the remotest chance that our friend here can understand us if we speak English?"

"English?" cried M d'Arvor. "Of course, he doesn't know a word. But why?"

"Oh well, just this—I think I know why he wants to get rid of us."

"You know?" said d'Arvor and Colebroke together.

Mr Pinson nodded. "There's something behind those panels which he is afraid to reveal."

M d'Arvor burst into a loud roar of laughter.

"I should think there is!" he exclaimed. "My dear Mr Pinson— you do not know the Breton *lit close*? The bedplace in the wall? Behind those panels are Madame Yves, and Madame Mère, an old lady of ninety, and Mademoiselle Yves, and three young rascals of boys. All the family of Yves, in fact. I should think he would be afraid to reveal it all—and it would embarrass us a little!"

"Ah," said Mr Pinson. "Pardon my stupid ignorance. Then, there will naturally be no room for us?"

"Not in the *lits closes*—and I don't think you open-air Englishmen would like to sleep in them—one feels like a sardine in a tin. But Yves has a fine roomy loft where we can sleep till morning. I don't know why he made any difficulty. But that is all over. We are going up. He will find some blankets, and there is plenty of dry hay."

Mr Pinson yawned very heartily.

"I shall be glad to get to sleep, my dear monsieur," said he. "We have had a very long day. But I simply cannot endure the smell of hay. I get fever. If you will arrange with our friend Yves to let me stay here, I will stretch out in the big chair there. You go on with Colebroke."

The arrangement was explained to the farmer. He scratched his head and seemed inclined to make further objection, but M d'Arvor became peremptory. Colebroke and d'Arvor followed him up the steep ladder in one corner of the room, and Pinson was left to himself.

"I say, Monsieur d'Arvor," he called as they disappeared, "I suppose I may put out the lamp? Ask him, will you? I cannot sleep if the room is lit."

"All right," the reply came after some murmuring overhead.

"And keep him up there with you," Pinson called.

"What's that?" asked M d'Arvor, coming to the trap door.

"Don't let him come down again," said Mr Pinson. "I'm all right."

Mr Pinson, in fact, was no longer sleepy. The disappearance of his friends seemed to lift the weight of slumber off his eyelids. Having waited until the footsteps in the loft had ceased, he went through some rapid movements. First, apparently lest any interruption to his repose should come from above, he stole quickly to the corner and removed the ladder out of reach of the manhole. He stood on a chair and extinguished the lamp. The room was now in deep gloom with only a tiny glow of light from the ember fine.

Mr Pinson cast a rapid glance along the two rows of panels, and listened. Now that there were no other sounds, deep breathing could be heard. There was even a snore....

Mr Pinson moved quietly to one panel in particular that seemed to exercise his curiosity. While M d'Arvor and Yves had argued and disputed, he had measured several times the glance the farmer gave so often along that wall and marked where it paused.

Mr Pinson stopped at that point and listened. Then he smiled to himself in the darkness.

He tapped two or three times on the panel with his finger nail. The sound could not be heard except by anyone within.

"Qu'est—ce que c'est?"

The voice was not raised above a whisper.

"You can come out," Mr Pinson whispered, using English. "Come out. I want to talk to you."

He spoke confidently, knowing that she would come out.

The panel slid quietly back, and a woman's figure emerged. Pinson put his hand over her mouth to enjoin silence, and pointed towards the door.

"Go out," he said, in her ear. "I will follow."

He returned to the corner, restored the ladder to its proper position, and tiptoed out of the room into the yard. There was a gleam of dawn in the sky. The fog had thinned. The woman awaited him, shivering. He caught her by the arm and walked her away through the wide gateway and along the rough road that ran through the bottom of the valley.

"Now, mignonne," said he, "you shall tell me exactly what happened in that quaint little English town of Longbridge on the night of the 18th of March, is it not so?"

"Mon dieu, monsieur!—what do you mean? What do I know of Longbridge or the 18th of March?"

Pinson stopped short in the road.

"Great heavens!" he said. "Can it be possible that I have made a mistake? Am I not talking to Madame Leduc, of The Cedars? What a ghastly error! A thousand apologies. Let us go back at once, and I will explain to M d'Arvor how grotesquely we have been misinformed, and we will all apologise to you, including Mr Colebroke."

He caught her arm as if to drag her back to the farmhouse.

"Ah no—no, no!" she cried. "Who are you, monsieur? You are terrible, relentless..."

She faced him in the twilight, panting.

"Oh, come now," said Mr Pinson. "Surely you do me an

injustice! Remember what happened up there." He jerked his head in the direction of the wooded hill that gloomed to the south. "I think you might be a little more candid, Madame Leduc. I only want to ask you a few simple questions."

She turned and walked on, Mr Pinson by her side.

PART 4 A RECONSTRUCTION

I

The packet boat had left Dieppe more than an hour. It was out of the green water into the blue. The French shore had disappeared, the English was not in sight.

Mr Pinson opened his eyes and stared into a dazzling sky. He stretched himself lazily in his deck chair and turned on his elbow to look at the man who lay in the chair beside him asleep.

Mr Pinson communed with himself.

A good-looking fellow, this Westmore Colebroke. No doubt of it. You wanted a little time to get accustomed to the beard. Beards were not very common nor at all liked in the Temple. You really could not afford to wear a beard till you reached the Bench. So one always associated beards with age—or something over middle age—and they were usually stiff and grizzled mats on hard skin. Hateful! But if you threw your mind back to your extreme youth and remembered the 'eighties, and Lord Randolph Churchill, and the "dudes" who sometimes wore beards...

Anyhow, Colebroke's beard was not like the beards you saw on careless old KCs or stuffy judges. It was a dark brown beard of soft hair and it grew on a skin of the clearest, purest complexion, with a flash of colour in it, skin without a wrinkle or a flaw. The eyebrows were arched, the forehead broad and fine. This artist was a solicitor—living on the grubby law! This solicitor at any rate was an artist.

Mr Pinson's communion broke off into an apostrophe to the sleeping man.

"Well, Colebroke, I must say you're a quixotic idiot and you've cost lots of worthy people heaps of trouble, including my worthy self. But I'm really not greatly surprised at Miss Maud. If I were a girl and twenty years younger, I might fall in love with you myself and risk the beard."

This Colebroke fellow, going about doing Sir Galahad stunts, rescuing fair damsels in distress, acting the preux chevalier, the very perfect gentle Knight! In his sleep he looked so young and innocent, so triumphantly healthy and so very English in spite of the beard. He was tall and slim, well made, alert; he looked an athlete: he was probably a fencer.

"It ought not to be allowed, you know, Colebroke. It's not fair to other men. Here you are, with all these damned good looks, all these quixotic virtues, all this strength, all these brains, and all the money a man can want—every confounded thing! Where do the others come in? Where should even I come in if I were twenty years younger and wanted Miss Elburton for myself?"

As Mr Pinson mused, Westmore Colebroke stirred, immediately sat bolt upright, and laughed to his companion out of dark brown eyes.

"Motion of the boat, I suppose," he said. "I've had forty winks."

"And the rest," said Mr Pinson. "We're half way over."

Colebroke sat looking at him steadfastly. It was a rather disconcerting trick of his.

"Anything wrong with my tie?" Mr Pinson asked.

"Apologies, my friend," Colebroke laughed. "I did not mean to be rude. I was only thinking what a topping chap you've been to dear old Elburton."

"I'm delighted," said Mr Pinson," to find someone at last who realises my profound merits. I've been thinking what a topping chap you haven't been to dear old Elburton. Dear old Elburton has been frightened out of his senses about you. He is now. He is mourning you dead, my dear Don Quixote."

Colebroke got up and took a hasty turn across the deck.

"Yes—but, Pinson, I was quite ignorant of all this, you know. And when I wanted to wire to him yesterday you wouldn't let me."

"Quite so. Reasons of state. Reasons of justice. Anything you like. Only I want to be in Longbridge before the truth gets out—or your part of it—in order to confirm what I believe to be the ultimate truth and to cut this frightful business short. Colebroke—you know our friends the police in those parts, and you'll admit that it's not an affair they can handle quietly."

"Very well—I've agreed. You have a theory and you want to confirm it. A day more or less won't matter. I've agreed."

"There is one thing I should greatly like to know," said Mr Pinson. "What do you make of our friend Yves? Was he in it? And what happened in the four days you were kicking your heels in that valley?"

"Yves was in it, undoubtedly. He kept me concealed in that beastly chapel two days and three nights in the expectation of seeing a lady who, he said, had sailed from Westport and was to be brought to me there in secret. It was the fog that caused the delay. Moreau dared not come by the little steamer to Morlaix. He came in a crab-boat he had hired—lots of French crabbers fish off the western coasts—and they were becalmed for two days. I have no doubt they landed on the coast near Locquirec the night you arrived."

Mr Pinson nodded.

"But as Yves was in it, you must have smelt a rat before the end?"

"Yes, of course. The last day he was so fidgety and worried that he almost gave himself away. I had made up my mind that there was a catch somewhere. You remember my very curt reception of yourself? But I intended to see it through—just in case, you know."

Mr Pinson looked inquisitively into Colebroke's face.

"You know, Colebroke, I don't believe you're a bit sorry that Mr Antoine Moreau got away."

"Well, I'm not. I bear no malice to Moreau. He behaved like a cad; but no worse than thousands of others. Custom of the country, you know. I hate and abominate it, Pinson. But I'm not going to preach to you."

"No; better not," said Mr Pinson dryly. "But behaving like a cad and attempting murder are two rather different matters."

Colebroke planted himself in front of Mr Pinson's chair.

"Look here, Pinson—you have a theory and you want to work it out. I leave it to you since you desire it. But until I know what it is the whole thing is dark to me. Will you tell me this: do you believe Antoine Moreau tried to murder me, as he thought, or procured any such attempt?"

Mr Pinson with great deliberation pulled out his cigarette-case and his match-box and prepared to smoke.

"Without giving away my theory prematurely," he said, "I can't answer that question." He lit his cigarette. "It was exactly the question which I had in mind to ask you. And now you have answered it. You don't believe it."

"I do not."

"Then who did?"

"I don't know."

"I think Monsieur d'Arvor believes it."

"Oh, Lucien!" said Colebroke with a shrug. "Lucien's a great fellow, but where I'm concerned he loses his head. And he doesn't know Moreau as I do."

"Well, my dear Colebroke," said Pinson, getting up from his chair and looking over the rail, "isn't that Eastbourne away to the right—and don't I see the hole where Newhaven is hiding? We'd better be packing up. I think you said you're not well known in London? Good."

II

On Thursday evening, Mrs Pinson and Miss Elburton sat in the tiny drawing-room of the Adelphi flat. The honourable Dora had been disposed of for the night. Irene had laid the table for three in the dining-room according to instructions. It was after seven. Dinner was to be at eight.

They were discussing the everlasting question of the Longbridge affair. The papers of the previous day had reported the preliminary police hearing of the charge against Mrs Findlater, that she was an accessory after the fact of the murder of Westmore Colebroke. Mrs Findlater, it seemed, had been remanded for a week after the production of some very sketchy evidence.

"Isn't it strange," asked Miss Elburton, "that no word has come from Mr Pinson? He will hardly keep his appointment for dinner."

"My dear," said Mrs Pinson, "you really know nothing about that eccentric husband of mine—nothing. If he said he would be here to dinner at eight, depend on it he will be here and pour floods of sarcasm on our domestic economy if the soup is not on the table as the clock strikes."

"And," said Miss Elburton, with knitted brows and a little flush in her cheeks, "is he to be depended upon to keep all his promises? You recall that he said he would have the secret out by now and that it would prove to be no secret at all."

"I think, my dear," said Mrs Pinson, "that he must have known a good deal about it when he spoke. He does the most surprising things—oh, the most surprising. He ought to have been a stage manager."

"Oh, I think he's wonderful," said the girl. "You could never believe how my father relied on him."

"Yes, I think I could, Maud. I remember how he spoke of your father when he received his letter."

"Wonderful!" she repeated.

Mrs Pinson smiled upon her.

"I suppose it's always the way. We all have the most wonderful men, don't we? You won't make Mr Colebroke jealous, by any chance—or me?"

"Oh, Mrs Pinson!" cried the girl. "I can't talk of Westmore. He's ———"

"Of course he is. I'm sure of it. I expect my eccentric husband has been busy making his acquaintance."

"You don't think——"

Miss Elburton left the question incomplete.

"No, it's better not to think too much. And here's half-past seven. I'll just go and have a look at the table."

Mr Pinson's stage-management was excellent. So natural that when he walked into the flat and told his driver to drop the suitcase, he seemed to have reached home from some unimportant visit.

"Tell Mrs Pinson I'm home, Irene," he said. "I'm going to change, and I'll look into the drawing-room for a minute before dinner. Miss Elburton here? Good."

Joyful noises from the bathroom and an interval of quiet preceded Mr Pinson's appearance before the two women, one of whom smiled indulgently upon him, and the other was bursting with repressed excitement.

"Good evening, Mrs Pinson. Good evening, Miss Elburton. Dinner nearly ready? I'm a wolf. I'm famished. Dora gone to bed, of course? Now then, stir up Irene, or I shall become a cannibal and start on you two. Eh? No questions—no cross-examination. The brute demands to be fed."

They let him have his way and fell in with his humour. Over dinner he steered them clear of the Longbridge mystery, declaring that he had never heard of it, and did not believe there was such a place as Longbridge. But after dinner they might try to persuade him that there was if they liked.

Mrs Pinson was about to give the signal to Miss Elburton.

"Do you mind," Mr Pinson asked, "having your coffee with me here and a cigarette? I'm replete—gorged—satisfied—lazy—don't want to move."

They kept their seats.

"Now, about this Longbridge mystery. I don't believe it. There's no mystery. It's all plain as Pinson."

"But have you seen that a woman has been arrested as an accomplice after the fact?" his wife asked.

"No! She can't be if there's no fact, can she? However, I thought they would. It's just what they would do. They've got to release her, that's all. About tomorrow, I should think. No time tonight. And another night away from the arms of the cupidinous Findlater won't do her any harm."

"Ah—so you know all about Mrs Findlater then?" cried Mrs Pinson.

"My dear girl—all! I hope not. But I know enough about her to be quite sure that the police have made a bloomer. Come, now—isn't that enough about the greengroceress? Hush!—what's that I hear?"

Mr Pinson rose, went round to his wife, and placed his hand on her shoulder. She gave him a quick look of understanding.

"Somebody's playing our piano," he said. "Well I'm——"

Miss Elburton regarded them both with a mystified stare. All three listened. The piano was being played softly. Then the notes of a baritone reached them, and faintly the words—

"Lorsque j'entends les doux murmures
De leurs printanieres chansons,
Je vas guetter, sous les ramures,
Les fauvettes et les pinsons . . ."

"I wonder," said Mr Pinson, "if Miss Elburton would mind going to see who it is taking liberties with our drawing-room?"

He kept his hand hard-pressed on Mrs Pinson's shoulder.

The girl paled, then flushed red, looked an instant into his smiling face, cried a little "Oh!" and ran from the room.

III

"It is Colebroke," said Mr Pinson.

"Idiot!" said his wife, holding him at arm's length.

"Yes, he is a bit of a fool, but a rather nice fool," said Mr Pinson.

"Idiot!" said Mrs Pinson again.

"Give them ten minutes," he answered, "to get over their idiotic raptures. Then I'll introduce you to the Longbridge mystery. And afterwards, the band will play—I assure you, Mrs Pinson, that the band will play. Pity the flat is so small; I doubt whether it will hold all the performers."

"Idiot!" cried Mrs Pinson.

"When I say it three times, it's true," Mr Pinson quoted. "But perhaps you will explain yourself."

"I should think, Noel, that it is from the eminent counsel for the defence that the explanation is due. Stop fooling, and tell me what you mean."

"No, absolutely not—absolutely and finally not, Mrs Pinson. The facts shall all come out in their proper order—and only once. I can't stand telling it all twice over. When we have given them their ten minutes, we will go in and resume the little talk where we left it on Monday evening. In the meantime, have some more coffee. I want to give Irene a hint."

At nine o'clock, Mr Pinson made an alarming noise outside the door of the drawing-room, cursing and kicking a non-existent cat, and then he and his wife went in.

Mrs Pinson saw a tall bearded young man sheltering Miss Elburton under his arm.

"Lor' bless my soul!" cried Mr Pinson, "if it isn't Colebroke—the mystery man! And he's deluded Miss Elburton into believing in him! And—oh, Mrs Pinson . . . Colebroke; Colebroke . . . know Mrs Pinson. Speak nicely to the lady—it's her piano, you know."

Mrs Pinson shook hands with him.

"You'll pardon my fatuous husband when you've known him as long as I have," she said. "How splendid!" She included Miss Elburton in the eulogium.

"Westmore has been telling me a little, Mr Pinson. We can never thank you enough."

"No, of course not," said Mr Pinson. "My deeds are only exceeded by the beauties of my character, and a library would not hold them all. So don't begin. Have a little more music? No? Shall we go out and give you another ten minutes? No? . . ."

"Idiot!" said Mrs Pinson.

"Ah well, Colebroke and I understand each other. We're both

lawyers. And I told him of that sitting of the court held here on Monday night and adjourned to the present evening. So if you've all had enough music and things, what do you say to beginning the proceedings? Mrs Pinson, preside. Miss Elburton, be seated. Colebroke, anything you say will be taken down in evidence. Sit on that settee; there's room for two. I want the other two chairs. That'll do."

IV

"I am now going," said Mr Pinson, "to explode the Longbridge mystery. I hope there will be no unseemly interruptions."

Mr Pinson handed a cigarette-box to Colebroke and began to smoke himself, speaking between his puffs.

"The Longbridge mystery," he said, "is over there on the settee beside Miss Elburton. I am about to expose him. If my biographical sketch is wrong in any particular, he will correct me. In the first place, he is an artist masquerading as a lawyer. In the next place, he is a crank. In the third place—and I beg you to note the importance of this—he is a puritanical crank. I should have liked to know his father. His father must have been a very remarkable man, for he was an excellent lawyer who knew how to make money and preserve the respect of his fellow men, and at the same time to bring up with a liberal education a congenitally pious and puritan son. Yes, Colebroke senior must have been worth knowing..."

Mr Pinson blew some smoke-rings.

"He found the youth he had on his hands a hard case. Instead of developing as the son of a lawyer should, all brains and no emotions, this youth displayed an extraordinary tenderness towards the arts. True, he had brilliant brains as well as sensitive perceptions. Colebroke senior, however, did what not one British father in a thousand would have dared to do. Instead of Eton and Oxford, to crush out the pernicious artistic tendencies of his offspring, he prescribed Paris for him. Paris! Where he was to learn as much law as he could contain and cultivate his emotions at the same time. Colebroke senior was a man of knowledge and character. He knew his Paris and had married a Parisienne—Colebroke's mother was French. He is, I am told, very like his mother in appearance.

"So we have this youth in Paris, working pretty hard at the law and other things, and enjoying the society of Bohemia, doing as the Bohemians do in nearly every particular, but not in two important ones. Strange apparition in Bohemia, this young Puritan who was nice to fastidiousness, in his abstemious habits, and had a poisonous hatred for light conduct towards women or light talk about them.

"Now we can cut a lot of cackle and come to the 'osses. Shortly before the war he made the acquaintance of Antoine Moreau, who was an ardent young politician of the Right and a violent critic of the powers in France. In one of those mushroom leagues young Frenchmen love he was associated with Monsieur Lucien d'Arvor, a close friend of Colebroke's, and a crowd of other artists, journalists, politicians and young men about town. Colebroke, being a sensible fellow on the whole, did not trouble about their politics. Moreau was an acquaintance only; there was no friendship between them.

"Then came the war...

"During the war, Colebroke, who was a liaison officer, met Moreau once only. After the war he met him only once more. But the Puritan in Colebroke was grossly offended by some facts that came to his knowledge about Moreau. In the early part of the war, when there were a good many ladies about behind the lines, Colebroke was nursed in hospital by a young English girl, and got to know something of her family. He gave her some good advice about going home to England, but did not know whether she took it or not. After the war, he found that she was in Paris, and was shocked to discover that she had a liaison with Antoine Moreau.

"Then the Puritan saw red, and was not content until he had broken up the tie, persuaded the young lady of her folly, and finally got her to return to her friends. Mr Moreau, not being a

Puritan, and not having the ghost of a notion what it meant to be a Puritan, was even more shocked than Colebroke had been; he was fully convinced that a man would interfere in such a matter only for one reason, and that was to get the girl for himself.

"While Colebroke was engineering Miss Vincent out of his clutches, Moreau was arrested for complicity in some absurd political plot. The police called Colebroke to give evidence of the one occasion on which he had seen Moreau since the war—an evening when he met him at the Café Boucher in a dirty little street off the Marché St Honoré. It was a purely formal piece of testimony. As Colebroke left the court, Moreau called him several pet names—such as traitor, coward, and filthy scoundrel—and nobody could understand this display of affection, so disproportionate to the occasion, except those who knew that Colebroke had pinched the gentleman's best girl. Moreau went to prison for two years.

"Shortly afterwards, Colebroke's father died, and he went to take up the practice at Longbridge. Next, the young English lady of whom he had deprived Moreau was very happily married, without a breath of scandal. Nobody knew anything about the episode in Paris. And then Colebroke made the acquaintance of my friend Elburton—mainly, it would seem, because he had a very charming daughter.

"I think most of the essential facts about that acquaintance are known to the court, so I need not labour them.

"Just before the time when Moreau came out of prison—when everybody had forgotten all about Moreau—Colebroke and Miss Elburton had jointly and severally made up their minds that they were absolutely necessary to each other's existence, if only because nobody in Longbridge could sing French songs except Colebroke and nobody could play the accompaniments like Miss Elburton. There were doubtless other reasons, which we need not explore.

"They were just about to communicate this momentous discovery to Mr Elburton when Colebroke received a letter from his friend d'Arvor telling him that Moreau was out of gaol, that he was still frantic about the abduction of his English miss, and was going about breathing fire and slaughter against Colebroke. As the French court had decided that after he came out of gaol France would be all the better for Mr Moreau's absence for a period of three years, he was exiled, and of course there was a possibility that he would choose this land of the free as his place of exile. Half in joke, d'Arvor warned Colebroke to be on the qui vive for his enemy.

"And almost simultaneously, Colebroke learnt that a certain house in Longbridge, The Cedars, had been taken by a French gentleman named Victor Leduc. He put two and two together. Then he decided to tell Miss Elburton the whole story under pledge of secrecy, to postpone the announcement to her father, and to disappear until something had happened to Mr Moreau. He kept in touch with Miss Elburton through his friend Lebaudy at Westport, but with nobody else in England. He had intended to tell Elburton a fairy tale about business abroad. But as things turned out, he had no time. The night when he left the Elburtons in Longbridge, he had meant to sleep quietly in his bed and the next day to call on Elburton and wish him goodbye. But something occurred between eleven o'clock and midnight which induced him to vanish without any explanation at all...

"And that's all I know about the Longbridge mystery," said Mr Pinson, reaching for another cigarette.

"Oh, but——" Mrs Pinson began.

"All I *know*, I said," Mr Pinson continued. "The rest I have guessed. I'm a regular dog at guessing. From this point forward, I will permit interlocutions where I go wrong. In the first place, Colebroke is a Quixotic lunatic."

"Wrong first time," said Colebroke.

"Very well," said Mr Pinson. "Then Colebroke is a staid and sedate solicitor, with all the qualifications demanded by the English Law Society and a French degree in Law as well, whose conduct throughout has been marked by the conventionality and sobriety proper to such a character. Have it as you like.

"Now, why did Colebroke decide to disappear? Was it because

he was afraid of Moreau and his threats? I think not. There were two reasons: one was that if he became involved in any collision with Moreau, that frantic idiot would be certain to make a public row about the young English miss, and tragedy would descend upon her life; the other was that any such business would be perfectly dreadful to Miss Elburton. That right?"

Colebroke nodded.

"Another rhetorical question. Did Colebroke imagine for a moment that Moreau would make any surreptitious attempt on his life or safety? Colebroke had no such idea. That right too?"

Colebroke nodded again.

"I think what Colebroke knew was that Moreau intended to challenge him to a duel, eh? Just as if they were in Paris and could find a corner in some Bois de Boulogne or Parc Monceau where they could wipe out each other's injuries and insults in blood. Is it not so?"

"I thought so," said Colebroke.

"Which was absurd and revolting to Colebroke's ideas. He could, of course, have put the police on Moreau's track—but there he was held up by his Quixotic anxiety for secrecy. Then, when he left Miss Elburton on the night of the 18th of March, he found, within half an hour or less, that the fire-eating Moreau had been too quick for him. He had already arrived in Longbridge. In point of fact he was at that very time waiting for Colebroke under the arches of the Town Hall. Colebroke saw a motor-car waiting near by, speculated curiously about it, and I can see what happened, but I cannot hear anything except two loud noises. Therefore I do not know what was said. Probably Moreau insisted on an appointment for a duel and Colebroke refused. Probably there was a row. At any rate, within a short time the guns went off by themselves. Colebroke was unhurt, but Moreau dropped. Then, before Colebroke could rush to the place where he had fallen, another man jumped out of the motor-car, also armed with a gun, and Colebroke dashed away into safety. I'm only guessing, but how's that?"

Colebroke nodded assent.

"After that, Colebroke was a bit scared. I don't know how he got there. But by one o'clock in the morning he was in Westport, and by two o'clock in the morning he was out in the English Channel on the little packet boat *Cornubia* that plies between Westport and St Brieux, and probably on the next day he was with his friend d'Arvor in Paris.

"I'm going," Pinson continued, "to put forward two hypotheses in which I don't believe much. One is that Colebroke did not know whether he had killed his man, and was nervous about it. The other is that he walked to Westport."

"Neither theory is well founded," said Colebroke. "I had no fear of having killed him because I had no weapon and therefore did not fire. And I didn't walk to Westport."

"Ah!" said Mr Pinson. "Then I am right. You supply me with the one missing link in my argument! Now I can tell you exactly what did happen.

While Moreau was quarrelling with you, your chauffeur Julep suddenly appeared as if from nowhere. He saw Moreau gesticulating with a pistol in his hand, and he pulled out a pistol and fired point-blank at your assailant, who fell back, but as he fell pulled his own trigger twice. The shots went over your heads. Then you and Julep had a conversation, after which you both went to the garage, and he drove you to Westport in your car. You stopped in the main street and saw that the body of Moreau had been removed and the motor-car had gone. I fancy you looked up, and though you saw no light in your windows, you probably concluded that the house must have been disturbed, and told Julep to get off as quickly as possible. You pledged him to complete secrecy about the whole affair and gave him a bank-note for a hundred pounds, and you promised him that later on when you came back you would re-engage him and overlook the indiscretion for which you had discharged him. How about that for a theory?"

"I suppose Julep has betrayed my confidence and told you the whole story," said Colebroke.

"On the contrary," said Mr Pinson, "I have never seen Julep in my fife yet, though I hope soon to have the pleasure of meeting him."

"Then I can't understand how you have worried it out."

"My dear Colebroke, the whole thing is as simple as my own childish character. There's a cause concealed in every event, and you've only got to look at the event hard enough and long enough to discover what the cause is.

"I divine the solution of the Longbridge mystery with the aid of Miss Maud. She is as secret as the grave. But on the first evening of our meeting she gives the whole show away. Obviously head over ears in love with the undeserving Colebroke, she is not a bit worried about him—only about her father. So it is clear that she knows where Colebroke is and is bound to keep the fact secret from her father, and therefore from me and everybody else. Dear little French songs, including the tune (but happily not the words) of that famous ditty 'Au clair de la lune.' Friendly with the little Frenchman Lebaudy. Lebaudy leads me to Boucher. Boucher to the Affaire Moreau. That to the files of the *Petit Parisien*. They scream out the dates. Then Grainger has been getting to work."

"Grainger?" cried Colebroke.

"Oh yes. I forgot I haven't told you about Grainger. Of course you know him—that most intelligent of ex-policemen?"

"Quite well."

"Grainger, of course, discovered your skeleton in the strong-room. But he discovered much more important things than that, it is true without realising their importance. He found Moreau's traces at The Cedars. And he blundered along in search of your murderer and turned up lots of useful people for me, including Mrs Findlater. Being perfectly sure that Julep had murdered you, he went ahead on that trail like a sleuth-hound. But knowing from Miss Elburton that the report of your murder was exaggerated, I kept on the Moreau trail, which ultimately led me to the Prefect of Police and M d'Arvor. M d'Arvor gave me a line on your character, and supplied the Quixotic motive—and consequently the explanation of your secrecy.

"M d'Arvor thought Moreau was murderous. But that was clearly not the fact. Anybody can murder anybody at any time, and if he had wanted to murder you, he would have done it. The duel—the outrage nursed in prison for two years, the imperative need to wipe it out in the approved fashion, the words 'à outrance' in one of the letters Grainger found at The Cedars: the determination of Moreau to fight a duel was established.

"Then there were the circumstances of the night of the 18th of March: the two shots which were heard and mistaken for back-fires, your sudden disappearance. I saw that Moreau had forestalled you, and that there had been a rough house that night. Dear old Grainger thought the shots were fired in your office. I knew they were fired from the outside. The bullet-mark on the panel of your strong-room was too high to have been fired from the room. And it had struck a slat of the Venetian blind as it came through. I measured it off and found the only spot in the street from which it could have been fired. It was a spot some two feet above the ground under the arches of the Town Hall. Therefore it was fired by a man either recumbent or falling. Couldn't arrive at any other conclusion, could one?"

"But," said Mrs Pinson, "if Moreau was killed in the street at Longbridge and both Mr Colebroke and his chauffeur fled to Westport, how did Moreau's body get into the strong-room in Mr Colebroke's office?"

V

"Ah!" said Mr Pinson, in response to his wife's question, "if anybody can tell me how the body of Antoine Moreau got into Mr Colebroke's strong-room, I shall be greatly obliged. But I perceive it is now close on half-past nine, and I have invited a friend to meet me here at half-past nine. He will be here in a minute or two. It is your old crony Grainger, Mrs Pinson."

Colebroke looked puzzled.

"Oh yes, I know Mr Grainger very well," said Mrs Pinson. "We were all three mixed up in an affair that happened some years ago in Devonshire."

"Can't stop to tell you about it now, Colebroke," Mr Pinson went on. "But I want you to do me a favour—and that is to get into the dining-room before Grainger comes. I want to teach Grainger a lesson. He's an excellent chap, but in this business he has been too much the policeman. He was bull-dosed at Scotland Yard by Sir—— But perhaps I won't mention any names, and though I warned him off the trail he was chasing he was so confoundedly dogmatic about it... However, let me take him in hand. The ladies are to say nothing in his presence of any of the facts I have mentioned this evening. Agreed? Then, I hear the punctual Grainger at the door. Colebroke, allez!"

A minute later, Mr Grainger was ushered into the room by Irene. He greeted Mrs Pinson as an old friend, and expressed surprise and delight that Miss Elburton looked so well.

"Ah, Grainger," said Mr Pinson. "I see you've laid the lovely Bella by the heels, and I suppose by this time you've found Julep?"

Mr Grainger shook his head despondently.

"No, Mr Pinson, unfortunately we have not. We have been hot on his trail, but every time he eludes us. The evidence is being piled up. We could slip the noose over his neck all right if we could catch him."

"Oh?" said Mr Pinson. "Anything new found since I saw you?"

"Yes; we've got a man who saw Julep and some other person that night in the neighbourhood of Mr Colebroke's house—hurrying away from it, as a matter of fact. Julep had an accomplice. That makes us all the more certain of getting him."

"Ah, very interesting, Grainger," said Mr Pinson. "The way you build up a case is really extraordinary."

Mr Grainger looked doubtfully at him, as though he caught an intonation not quite sincere.

"Don't want any bouquets, Mr Pinson," said he. "There's not much to brag about so far, is there? But how about you? Found anything? You didn't ask me to come down this evening for nothing, I'm sure."

"Well—no, I didn't. But excuse me a moment, I think I hear somebody outside." Mr Pinson went to the door, met Irene in the tiny hall, and said a few words to her.

"Mr Grainger," he resumed. "I didn't ask you to come for nothing. I think I've turned up a person you will be surprised and delighted to see.... Will you come in?"

Mr Pinson addressed this question to the outer air. A clean-shaven man entered the room, holding his hat between his hands, and looked suspiciously round.

A little cry of astonishment burst from Miss Maud.

"Don't be nervous," said Mr Pinson. "Come in. I'll introduce you. Miss Elburton you know." The man touched his forelock. "This is my wife, Mrs Pinson. And this is Mr Grainger who is a well-known detective in Westport and is interested in the Longbridge case."

The man gave a long look at Mr Grainger.

"Now," said Mr Pinson, "you all know each other."

"Pardon me," Mr Grainger remarked, "but I have not the pleasure of knowing your visitor."

"Oh no, of course! How stupid. You have never seen him before. Nor have I, for that matter," said Mr Pinson. "But I think I shall not be far wrong if I take upon myself to introduce you. Mr Grainger, this is Mr Julep. Mr Julep, will you be good enough to know Mr Grainger?"

While Mrs Pinson expelled a gasp of surprise, Mr Grainger leapt to his feet, opened his mouth to speak, failed to articulate anything, looked from the man who stood twirling his hat to Mr Pinson, and from Mr Pinson back again to the man, and then sank into his seat. Mr Pinson smiled. Mr Grainger then recovered his power of speech.

"A joke is a joke, Mr Pinson," said he. "But this is carrying a joke too far."

"Joke? I know I am credited with a lively sense of humour, Grainger: but where is the joke?"

"Do you mean to ask me to believe this man is Julep?"

"Ask him yourself."

"Are you Julep?" Mr Grainger shot the question at him.

"Yes," said the man.

"You know there is a warrant out for the arrest of William Julep on a charge of murdering Mr Westmore Colebroke at Longbridge on the 18th of March?"

"Yes, I know."

"And you still say you are William Julep?"

"No doubt whatever about it."

"Then," said Mr Grainger, "I arrest you, William Julep, on the charge of being concerned in the murder of Mr Colebroke, and ———"

"And anything he says may be taken down in writing and given in evidence against him on his trial," Mr Pinson put in. "Julep knows all about that, Grainger, but he's willing to bet you all Lombard Street to a china orange that he is neither arrested not tried."

"Arrested he is," said Mr Grainger stubbornly.

"Nothing of the kind, Grainger. Don't be an ass. You know me better—or you ought to. I told you that you were on the wrong trail."

"I have arrested him," Mr Grainger persisted.

"You said you had, but you haven't, you know. You're not going to make yourself the laughing stock of the whole country if I know it. Take it from me that Julep had nothing whatever to do with the murder of Mr Colebroke."

"I can't, Mr Pinson. The evidence is too strong."

"You won't take it even from me?" asked Mr Pinson.

"No, sir, not even from you."

"Very well, then, Grainger. For your obstinacy I ought to let you go on with your scheme, put an end for ever to your career as a detective, and destroy your character as a man of common sense. But for the sake of my friend Mrs Grainger, and the memory of all the cups of tea she has given me, I won't. I'll blow your evidence to smithereens in half a dozen words. Julep had nothing to do with the murder of Mr Colebroke because Mr Colebroke has not been murdered."

Mr Grainger clutched at his collar.

"Am I dreaming?" he faltered. "Or is this a lunatic asylum?"

"You are only half asleep," said Mr Pinson, "and this is my drawing-room. Allow me."

He stepped to the dining-room door, opened it and beckoned. Mr Grainger saw a tall dark bearded man come in, who looked at him an instant, and then walked across, saying;

"Hullo, Mr Grainger! Whoever would have thought of meeting you here?"

VI

When Mr Grainger saw Westmore Colebroke, whose corpse he had discovered in the strong-room at Longbridge, holding out his hand and heard his greeting, he uttered a cry of dismay.

"Now," said Mr Pinson, "perhaps you'll withdraw the slander you have put on Mr William Julep, and apologise to him."

Mr Grainger looked helplessly round at the group.

"Of course," he groaned. "'Smithereens,' you said. But I must confess, Mr Pinson, that you haven't been very kind to me."

"No," Mr Pinson answered. "I have not. I have been deliberately unkind. And I'll tell you why, Grainger. Do you remember what I said to you when you got in with the Scotland Yard crowd? I warned you. I could not be very explicit. There was a deep need for secrecy. But by going over to them and taking up their precious clues, you gave me a lot of unnecessary trouble. I'm simply paying you out for that. I wanted your help in the specific job of protecting the interests of Mr Elburton. You were scared off it on to the police track by the grisly discovery you made in the strong-room at Mr Colebroke's office."

"Ah—so you admit I didn't imagine that?" cried Grainger. "That wasn't a dream? There was a corpse?"

"Undoubtedly there was. You showed it to me."

"And if a corpse, therefore a murder. If not Mr Colebroke, then somebody else! Who?"

"My dear Grainger—all things in due order, and no rushing

to conclusions. First we will dispose of your suspicions about Julep, which put you on the wrong trail, and correct your rush to the conclusion that Mr Colebroke had been murdered. I never believed that Mr Colebroke had been murdered. I never believed Julep had anything to do with whatever happened in Mr Colebroke's office. You drew your conclusions about Julep from the suspicions created by gossip and from the letters of Mr Colebroke and Bella Waters which were to me the staring proof of his innocence."

"Why!" cried Grainger, "those were the very letters in which Mr Colebroke accused him of lying and Bella Waters referred to the money stolen from Mr Colebroke!"

"Too fast, too fast, my dear Grainger! You did not read between the lines, and you overlooked the significance of the dates. Mr Colebroke dismissed Julep for eavesdropping. His letter refusing to take Julep back was dated 16th March. If Julep could produce evidence by the following day of his innocence, he was to receive ample compensation. The following day was the 17th. The letter in which Julep sent a sum of money to Bella Waters was written on the 18th. The 18th was the day when Mr Colebroke drew a large sum from his bank. We know that what Julep sent to Bella Waters was a note for £100, and that it was one of the notes drawn by Mr Colebroke. The money was sent before the murder was committed. How did you come to overlook that?

"Besides, Grainger, you know well enough that a murderer who has stolen money from his victim will endeavour to leave as few traces as possible. He always leaves some. But if Julep murdered and robbed anybody, he simply went about shouting the fact all over the place. If he had stolen that money he would probably not have sent it to Bella Waters at all. But he certainly would not do what he did—which was to take it to Longbridge Post Office, enclose it in a registered envelope, and insure it, stating what it was! The morning before you and I opened the strong-room, I went to the Post Office and got the facts. So that I was perfectly certain that, whoever had committed a crime, it was not Julep.

"What had happened was evident. Julep had produced the evidence which Mr Colebroke believed to have no existence, and had received the substantial compensation—'amends,' I think the letter said. Then there remained the question why he had in such a hurry, on the day of Mr Colebroke's disappearance, sent this money to his girl in a letter which made some apparently confused allusions to the prospect that he would be away for an indefinite time. 'Indefinite time' gave it to me. Colebroke and Julep disappeared on the same day—indeed, almost at the same hour. If there had been no crime, and if they had been reconciled, I was driven to believe that they disappeared for the same cause. Then Julep knew why Mr Colebroke had gone, just as Miss Elburton knew."

"Miss Elburton knew?" echoed Grainger.

"Oh yes. I forgot that you don't know Miss Elburton knew, and she was pledged to secrecy. If she was pledged to secrecy, so was Julep. Julep would be very hard to find, for clearly he would not go near Bella Waters, and there was no other line on which to look for him.

"Then, Grainger, you put me on the right scent without knowing it. You were very clever to get that paper out of Bella Waters, and she was a minx to give it to you. You didn't understand it, but as soon as you read it to me—you know, the letter you thought was a blackmailing document—I could see through the whole thing. This was why Mr Colebroke had vanished: he was being threatened, and for one reason or another he did not want to meet the people who were threatening him.

"Why had Julep possession of this letter, and why did he send it to the woman? If Julep was innocent of crime, the only possible theory was that Colebroke had passed it to him for safe keeping, to be produced if occasion required, and he had chosen this obscure way of banking it. I could not see motive for all this, only the facts.

"So, my dear Grainger, when you and I stood with Elburton in that terrible room, I was quite aware, first that Julep had not committed a murder, and secondly that the body you found was not Colebroke's. And that simplified things enormously."

"I'm all in the dark still," said Grainger. "There was a body. Whose body was it? And who killed him?"

"Ah," said Mr Pinson, "that was a question for the police, not for me. All I wanted was to find Colebroke and save the sanity of my friend Elburton."

"But—the body!" Mr Grainger persisted.

VII

Mr Pinson looked very steadily at Grainger for a few seconds, and then took a cigarette from his box and lit it.

"I expect you've been doing a bit of thinking, Grainger," he said. "Hasn't it dawned on you?"

"No—I've been listening, not thinking."

"Well," said Mr Pinson, with a shrug of his shoulders, "I don't know that it's any part of my business to solve the problems of the police. I do know whose body it is, or I can make a fair guess, and think I can reconstruct every essential fact in the history of the 18th March at Longbridge. I will try if Mr Colebroke and Julep will answer the questions I put to them. But mind you, Grainger, this is without prejudice to anybody. For the time you are not an agent of Scotland Yard but a guest of Mrs Pinson. Do you agree?"

"Naturally," said Mr Grainger.

"Then—Colebroke, do you know whose body was found in your strong-room at Longbridge?"

"No—I never knew there was a body till you told me yesterday. I was mewed up at Nôtre Dame de Secours for nearly a week, and had seen no papers."

"And—Julep, do you know?"

"No, sir," said Julep, "but I can guess."

"Very well. Colebroke, I shall not be far out in suggesting that the conversation which you thought Julep had overheard on the Tuesday evening—that would be the 15th March—was a conversation in your office between you and Mr Toms, your confidential clerk?"

"It was."

"Shall I be wrong in supposing that you had detected Mr Toms in dishonest practices, that you were loth to prosecute him because he had been long in the service of your father, but that you had told him he must go, and that on this particular night you were going through some of his books and papers with him?"

"That was the case."

"And that you believed nobody but yourself knew anything of the circumstances?"

"I thought that, certainly."

"And you came to know that Julep was aware of them, and believed that he could only have become aware by listening in some way to that conversation?"

"Yes, Julep said something to me about Toms which I believed he could have learnt only by eavesdropping."

"I don't know what it was," said Pinson.

"It doesn't matter much," Colebroke replied. "I had taken pity on Toms and given him a small sum of money to go away with. That was at the end of the interview. The next day Julep said when we were in the car that he heard Toms had gone, and declared that he was a lucky scoundrel to get off with fifty pound in his pocket instead of a flea in his ear. As the only persons who knew the amount were Toms and myself, and the only occasion when it was mentioned was at that interview, I drew my own conclusion."

"Now," said Pinson, "I will put it to Julep that he always had a lower opinion of Toms than Mr Colebroke held."

"Indeed I did, sir," said Julep. "I knew him for a waster. He drank on the sly. He was a punter on horses and carried on like a man that had plenty of money. That Tuesday night, he came blustering into the tap of the hotel and tried to get up a row with me, called me a lickspittle and a miser, and blew about his being off to London with fifty quid in his pocket to spend, and showed the notes. That stuck in my throat and made me say what I did to

Mr Colebroke."

"But Toms did not go to London, did he?"

"No, sir. He went to Westport. I saw him in the town on the Thursday evening, which was race day. Then I told Mr Colebroke a few things about him."

"And Mr Colebroke withdrew his notice of dismissal?"

"Not that day, sir; it was the Friday, the 18th. Can I tell him about it, Mr Colebroke?"

"Yes, have it all out," said Colebroke.

"Well, it was very much as you said, sir. In the afternoon, Mr Colebroke called me up and told me that he believed what I had said, and that he was very sorry he mistrusted me, and he gave me a hundred pound note. I said I didn't want it if he would keep me on. Then he told me that he was going away privately for an urgent reason, and didn't know when he would be back. I was to clean up in the garage and go away just as if the notice held good. But when he returned he would send for me. I was to give him an address. I gave him the only one I could think of—Bella's address at Shepherd's Bush.

"Then, sir, Mr Colebroke seemed to think very hard, and he says to me, 'Julep, can I trust you?' I said he could. Then he told me he was clearing out for a time to avoid some people who threatened him, and he wanted to have a letter kept in safety —not at Longbridge, but in private hands. It was a letter that would clear things up if anything happened to him. I suggested that I was going to send my money to Bella, and she would keep the letter too until I asked her for it. He thought that would do. If I heard of his death I was to get the letter and give it to Mr Elburton; if not, I was to return it to him when he came back. I sent off the letter and the money by that evening's post."

"Did you see Toms after the Thursday evening, when you noticed him in Westport?" asked Mr Pinson.

"I can't swear that I saw him, but I thought I did on the Friday."

"Ah," said Mr Pinson. "Now let me try to imagine what happened to you on the Friday evening—what it was that made you disappear from Longbridge that night and never appear in the place again. You had previously paid up your lodgings to Mrs Colwill, but had gone back in the afternoon to ask if she could put up with you for a few days longer. That was after Mr Colebroke had agreed to take you back. You meant to overhaul and lay up the car and perhaps to get a few small seeds sown in the garden?"

Julep nodded.

"Then you spent the later part of the evening in the taproom of the hotel. You left at ten o'clock. Then, I think, you went to the garage? Yes. You probably spent some time there. At any rate it was after eleven when you came to the corner of the street, intending to return to Mrs Colwill's house. I should suppose that you must then have seen the man whom you thought might be Toms. Did he not enter Mr Colebroke's house? I thought so. But as the servants had already gone to bed, the house must have been locked up. Therefore I imagine Toms must have had a latchkey. In fact, I know he had."

"He had," said Colebroke. "But how did you know he had?"

"All in good time," replied Mr Pinson. "But you, Julep, must have thought it was a strange thing for Toms, under the circumstances, to be going at that time of night into the house from which he had been dismissed. So you probably hung about to see what would happen."

"Yes," said Julep, "I stayed at the corner."

"And while you were waiting there, a motor car arrived and drew up just beyond the arches of the Market Hall. Probably you set up some sort of connection in your mind between the car and the man, thought to be Toms, who had gone into the house?"

"Yes, I thought it was a motor robbery stunt."

"Somebody got out of the car and went into the shadows behind the Market Hall pillars. He probably didn't see you."

"No, he didn't. I crouched back and watched."

"And then, Mr Colebroke came down the street. The pillars were between you and him, and before he got near you the man under the arches had stopped and challenged him. They had an altercation and you then rushed out and came up behind Mr

Colebroke. As you ran, did you see a light flash up in the window of Mr Colebroke's room? Yes, I thought so; you saw that Mr Colebroke's assailant was brandishing a revolver. You pulled out your own gun and over Mr Colebroke's shoulder you fired point blank into the face of the man."

"Yes, I did; I let him have it right in the eyes," said Julep with a grin.

"Hardly a laughing matter, I should think," said Mr Grainger.

"He fell," Mr Pinson pursued. "And as he fell, there were two shots from his pistol, which went over your heads. As he lay on the ground and a second man came running from the car, you and Mr Colebroke bolted off. You went to the garage, got out the two-seater, and drove by the by-roads to Westport, where you left Mr Colebroke. You returned to Longbridge, garaged the car, and then you too disappeared. On the journey to Westport you had probably discussed with Mr Colebroke what you should do, and he thought it would be better for you to go away and lie low until you heard from him."

"That's quite right so far as it goes," said Julep, "but it isn't quite all."

"No," said Mr Pinson. "There are one or two points not clear. When did you tell Mr Colebroke that the pistol you fired at his man was only the little ammonia squirt you carried to use on dogs?"

Julep grinned again.

"In the garage," he said. "Mr Colebroke was scared stiff at first, but when he heard he laughed fit to crack his sides. It was as good as a Colt; the man went down smack and I believe he thought he was shot."

"And," said Mr Pinson, "when you came back into the street, both the man and the car had gone? Very well. There's only one other thing of any consequence I can't understand, unless you, Colebroke, went into your house before you started for Westport."

"Well—I didn't. My one anxiety was to get away, and I suddenly thought of the boat. By hurrying I could just catch it."

"Then what about the money? You surely hadn't got three thousand pounds on you all the evening?"

"I surely had! The wad of notes was in my pocket-book, and had never been out of it since I got them from the bank."

"Ah, I see," said Mr Pinson. "That solves the last doubt in my mind. Now, Grainger, I will tell you the name of the man you found dead in Colebroke's strong-room, and how he came by his death."

VIII

"Of course," said Mr Grainger, "the man who was found dead in the strong-room was Toms. But how was he murdered, and by whom?"

In the first place, why did you rush to the conclusion that it was Colebroke—you and the police?"

"That was almost inevitable," Mr Grainger replied. "Colebroke was missing for three months. It was Colebroke's house. The man was wearing Colebroke's clothes. That the body should be Colebroke's was more than a hypothesis, Mr Pinson, you'll admit."

"Yes, perhaps. All the same, if I had not been convinced (as I was) that Colebroke was alive, I should have known when I saw that body that it was not Colebroke's. I knew at a glance that it was not Colebroke's."

"How did you know, Mr Pinson?"

"Because, although the clothes were Colebroke's, who gives away his old suits, the boots were certainly not. Boots are jolly good evidence, Grainger. The boots on that corpse were cheap boots that Colebroke would no more have thought of wearing that he would of going about in a two-guinea reach-me-down suit. It might be possible for somebody else to be wearing Colebroke's clothes, but absolutely impossible for Colebroke to be wearing anybody else's boots."

"H'm!" said Mr Grainger.

"Another question, Grainger. Why did you and the police rush to the conclusion that the man had been murdered?"

"What!" cried Mr Grainger. "You surely aren't going to suggest that he died a natural death?"

"No, but I am going to suggest, and to prove, that he killed himself," said Mr Pinson.

"Oh come, Mr Pinson! You know perfectly well that there was no weapon in the place with which he could possibly have killed himself. And what about the bullet I dug out of the panel? He couldn't have fired that at himself."

"Certainly not. But I told you just now, Grainger, that boots are jolly good evidence. You didn't look at his boots, and I did. That's where I have the advantage of you.

"Now, let us consider what Toms did that night—or what I am as certain he did as if I had seen him do it. Toms was a bad lot, as Mr Colebroke has told us. He was a worse lot than Mr Colebroke thought. My curiosity was first attracted to Toms, to whom nobody else seems to have given a thought, by something I found in his desk at Longbridge. I have it here," said Mr Pinson, pulling out a little penny memorandum book. "It is Mr Toms's betting book. A managing clerk who bets—and in large sums too —hum, hum! Well, it made me very curious about Mr Toms. As soon as he had left Mr Colebroke, he probably squandered that fifty pounds with the bookmakers at Westport races. Then he planned a robbery at Colebroke's house. He had a latch-key for office purposes. He had not given it up. I know he had a latchkey, because I picked it up in the strong-room myself, lying beside his head, and I afterwards tried it on Colebroke's door and found that it fitted. I will tell you in a minute, why I think that latchkey was not in his pocket but on the floor.

"Well, Toms got into the house, bent on robbery. He went upstairs to Mr Colebroke's room, and he opened the strong-room, pulled the door behind him without quite closing it, and switched on the light. He then went to work on that cash-box which we saw, and having forced it open, found that it contained no money. I think I can safely say that Colebroke never kept any money in that place. He will tell me if I am wrong."

"No," said Colebroke, "I never did."

"And the reason is obvious; the place could not be locked up. The only fastening was the lever latch hidden behind the panel. That was one of the curious things that struck me when we were there. Toms was disappointed, but had hardly time to swear at his luck before his attention was disturbed by the noise of a quarrel going on in the street outside. He pushed open the door of the strong-room and went to the window to see what was happening. I know he did that because when Julep went to Mr Colebroke's assistance he glanced up and saw a light in the office window. As Toms was looking into the street—and he could probably see nothing—two shots were fired, and the first of them came through the window next to him, the middle one of the three, which was open, crashed against the Venetian blind —and you dug it out of the panel three months afterwards.

"Then Toms, who had seen nothing but the flash of a shot, and thought he was being fired at, rushed back to the strong-room, turned in the doorway and in a frantic hurry pulled the door home with a bang. In that action, Toms killed himself. His toes were on the threshold. The huge iron door, pulled with great violence, crashed into and over them and pinned him in agony as he fell back on the floor."

"Stop, Pinson!" cried Colebroke.

Miss Elburton had collapsed on the settee, fainting.

Mr Pinson, who had been leaning forward and talking solely to Mr Grainger, jumped up greatly disturbed.

"I'm sorry," said he. "I'm afraid I forgot the ladies. Won't you take her into the next room?" he asked his wife. "We will finish this off quickly now."

Mrs Pinson helped the girl out of the room.

"You'll forgive me, Colebroke?" said Mr Pinson. "Perhaps it is as well they have gone. For what is to come is even more horrible."

"I don't see——" Grainger was beginning.

"Let me get it over," said Mr Pinson. "That unhappy man died the most shocking death that a man ever died. The police believe he was shot. I know he wasn't. The doctor had not completely examined the skeleton when the inquest opened. They will find no trace of a bullet-wound. Both Grainger and the police were prepossessed on this question; they had no doubt it was Colebroke and they had their bullet. They did not look for anything else. They found what they wanted to find. I knew it was not Colebroke, and I had already seen that the bullet came from outside the house.

"Also, the man's position, with his knees drawn up, showed me that he could not have been shot. He would have been lying prone. Then I looked at his boots, and saw that the toes for two inches were crushed flat. I closed the door upon him while Grainger was experimenting with his reconstruction of the shooting scene, and saw precisely what had happened. It was as I have told you. The flange of the door was an obtuse angle. It fitted over a little sloping sill of wood, and the man's feet were caught on this sill. How he died, from shock, agony or starvation, with the lever that would have let him out just above his eyes and no possibility of reaching it, I can't tell you. How long he took to die, I can't tell you. But there he died. He must have lived some.

"I said I would tell you why he took the latchkey out of his pocket. Have you ever heard of the thirst that comes of intense pain, and of men sucking steel to relieve their thirst?

"Now I propose," said Mr Pinson, "that we don't discuss this any more."

"For heaven's sake give me a drink!" said Mr Grainger.

"Righto, Grainger. And you won't forget to tell your friend Catlin to let Mrs Findlater out at once, will you?"

IX

Mrs Findlater had been let out. Mr Colebroke had made her acquaintance and had told her that she might keep the famous hundred-pound note as a solatium for the indignity she had suffered; he would see that Julep got another one. As for Julep, he long nurtured a mood of brutal misogyny. That is to say, he made an exception in favour of Rose, but on the sex at large he held the gloomiest and most sanguinary views.

As the puzzle of the strong-room had been solved without any arrest, and nobody had to he hanged, the solution was regarded by the public as an anti-climax, and it soon forgot all about Longbridge. So far as the public was concerned, indeed, it learnt very little at all. The police simply admitted the mistake of identity, and put forward the theory that Toms had entrapped himself by accident while engaged in a burglary. No need, therefore, for the public to know anything about M Antoine Moreau and his strange proceedings in England.

A month afterwards, Mr Pinson spent a weekend with his friend Elburton, and there was music in the drawing-room. Mr Pinson discovered how perfectly Miss Maud accompanied Colebroke's songs.

What interested him more was a letter which Colebroke had received from his friend d'Arvor.

"There is a quick sequel to the events of Nôtre Dame de Secours," said M d'Arvor. "Moreau's car was traced to a garage at Locquirec, where they had landed in the fog. It seemed that he hoped to get a sailing boat to take him back to England, but messieurs the agents were too fast for him. He was caught hiding in a cottage at Locquirec, and Lemaître (who passed as Leduc in England) was captured with him. Both of them were taken to Paris. Our friend the Prefect was greatly amused by the story, and (as he has rather old-fashioned opinions about the duel) he did not go to extremes with Moreau. He gave him twenty-four hours to leave the country on condition that he made no attempt to go back to England. So I suppose he is now languishing on the banks of Lake Geneva, or in some such place, and wondering after all whether it was worth while.

"Moreau seems to have had a bad quarter of an hour with an English apothecary who offended his nose with salts of ammonia. At least I hear he is very sore on the subject of ammonia. He hates that innocent chemical so much that he flies into madness if it is mentioned in his presence. I expect it is an obsession. I always thought he was a little mad.

"Give my most cordial salutations to Mr Pinson. I thought we knew something about blague in Paris, but he is the blagueur par excellence, eh?"

"He is a flatterer," said Mr Pinson. "I take myself very seriously, don't you think, Miss Maud?"

"I think you conceal your seriousness with great success, Mr Pinson. But I shall never feel very comfortable with a secret when you are in the same room," said Miss Elburton.

"I can assure you," he replied, "that you may have as many secrets as you like, and I will never give them away. For example, you and Colebroke intend to get rid of me and your father in about ten minutes, in order that he may tell you something and you may answer him back without interruption. But I won't say a word about it to anybody."

"Ass!" said Colebroke. "Get!"

"This is how he treats the hero who rescued him at midnight from the ruined chapel in the gloomy wood on the wild shore! Come along, Elburton. We'll get!"

FINIS

R.A.J. WALLING CRIME FICTION BIBLIOGRAPHY

1. *The Strong Room* (Jarrolds, London 1927/no US edition). Noel Pinson and Superintendent Joe Grainger series. Spitfire Publishers Ltd, 2023.
2. *The Dinner Party at Bardolph's* (Jarrolds, London 1927). US title: *That Dinner at Bardolph's* (William Morrow & Company, New York 1928).
3. *Murder at the Keyhole* (Methuen & Company, London 1929/ William Morrow & Company, New York 1929).
4. *The Man with the Squeaky Voice* (Methuen & Company, London 1930/William Morrow & Company, New York 1930).
5. *The Stroke of One* (Methuen & Company, London 1931/ William Morrow & Company, New York 1931).
6. *The Fatal Five Minutes* (Hodder & Stoughton, London 1932). US title: *The Fatal 5 Minutes* (William Morrow & Company, New York 1932). Philip Tolefree series, 1 of 22.
7. *Behind the Yellow Blind* (Hodder & Stoughton, London 1932). US title: *Murder at Midnight* (William Morrow & Company, New York 1932).
8. *Follow the Blue Car* (Hodder & Stoughton, London 1933). US title: *In Time for Murder* (William Morrow & Company, New York, January 1933). Philip Tolefree series, 2 of 22.
9. *The Tolliver Case* (Hodder & Stoughton, London 1934). US title:

Prove It, Mr. Tolefree (William Morrow & Company, New York July 1933). Philip Tolefree series, 3 of 22.

10. *Eight to Nine* (Hodder & Stoughton, London 1934). US title: *The Bachelor Flat Mystery* (William Morrow & Company, New York 1934). Philip Tolefree series, 4 of 22.

11. *The Five Suspects* (Hodder & Stoughton, London 1935). US title: *Legacy of Death* (William Morrow & Company, New York 1935). Philip Tolefree series, 5 of 22.

12. *The Cat and the Corpse* (Hodder & Stoughton, London 1935) US title: *The Corpse in the Green Pyjamas* (William Morrow & Company, New York 1935). Philip Tolefree series, 6 of 22.

13. *Mr Tolefree's Reluctant Witnesses* (Hodder & Stoughton, London 1936) US title: *The Corpse in the Coppice* (William Morrow & Company, New York 1935). Philip Tolefree series, 7 of 22.

14. *The Corpse in the Crimson Slippers* (Hodder & Stoughton, London 1936/William Morrow & Company, New York 1936). Philip Tolefree series, 8 of 22.

15. *The Corpse with the Dirty Face* (Hodder & Stoughton, London 1936) US title: *The Crime in Cumberland Court* (William Morrow & Company, New York 1936). Philip Tolefree series, 9 of 22. Later published as *The Crime in Cumberland Court* (Hodder & Stoughton, London 1938).

16. *The Mystery of Mr Mock* (Hodder & Stoughton, London 1937). US title: *The Corpse with the Floating Foot* (William Morrow & Company, New York 1936). Philip Tolefree series, 10 of 22.

17. *Bury Him Deeper* (Hodder & Stoughton, London 1937). US title: *Marooned with Murder* (William Morrow & Company, New York 1937). Philip Tolefree series, 11 of 22.

18. *The Coroner Doubts* (Hodder & Stoughton, London 1938). US title: *The Corpse with the Blue Cravat* (William Morrow & Company, New York 1938). Philip Tolefree series, 12 of 22.

19. *More than One Serpent* (Hodder & Stoughton, London 1938) US title: *The Corpse with the Grimy Glove* (William Morrow & Company, New York 1938). Philip Tolefree series, 13 of 22.

20. *Dust in the Vault* (Hodder & Stoughton, London 1939). US

title: *The Corpse with the Blistered Hand* (William Morrow & Company, New York 1939). Philip Tolefree series, 14 of 22.

21. *They Liked Entwhistle* (Hodder & Stoughton, London 1939). US title: *The Corpse with the Red-Headed Friend* (William Morrow & Company, New York 1939). Philip Tolefree series, 15 of 22.

22. *Why Did Trethewy Die?* (Hodder & Stoughton, London 1940). US title: *The Spider and the Fly* (William Morrow & Company, New York 1940). Philip Tolefree series, 16 of 22.

23. *By Hook or by Crook* (Hodder & Stoughton, London 1941). US title: *By Hook or Crook* (William Morrow & Company, New York 1941). Philip Tolefree series, 17 of 22.

24. *Castle-Dinas* (Hodder & Stoughton, London 1942). US title: *The Corpse with the Eerie Eye: A Philip Tolefree Mystery* (William Morrow & Company, New York 1942). Philip Tolefree series, 18 of 22.

25. *The Doodled Asterisk* (Hodder & Stoughton, London 1943). US title: *A Corpse by Any Other Name* (William Morrow & Company, New York 1943). Philip Tolefree series, 19 of 22.

26. *A Corpse Without a Clue* (Hodder & Stoughton, London 1944/ William Morrow & Company, New York 1944). Philip Tolefree series, 20 of 22.

27. *The Late Unlamented* (Hodder & Stoughton, London 1948/ William Morrow & Company, New York 1948). Philip Tolefree series, 21 of 22.

28. *The Corpse with the Missing Watch* (William Morrow & Company, New York 1949). No UK edition. Philip Tolefree series, 22 of 22.

Serial-Only Detective Novels

1. *The Fatal Glove*. Noel Pinson and Superintendent Joe Grainger series.
2. *The Fourth Man*. Noel Pinson and Superintendent Joe Grainger series.
3. *The Merafield Mystery*.
4. *The Third Degree*.

Printed in Great Britain
by Amazon